'If poetry was the supreme literary form of the First World War then, as if in riposte, in the Second World War, the English novel came of age. This wonderful series is an exemplary reminder of that fact. Great novels were written about the Second World War and we should not forget them.'

WILLIAM BOYD

'It's wonderful to see these books given a new lease of life [...] classic novels from the Second World War written by those who were there, experienced the fear, anguish, pain and excitement first-hand and whose writings really do shine an incredibly vivid light onto what it was like to live and fight through that terrible conflict.'

JAMES HOLLAND, Historian, author and TV presenter

'The Imperial War Museum has performed a valuable public service by reissuing these absolutely superb novels'

ANDREW ROBERTS, author of *Churchill: Walking with Destiny*

'This is an absolute gem. The attention to detail, the rising tension and the utterly convincing characters give this a flavour of very real and intense authenticity. As I read it, I became aware that this stunning short novel could only have been written by someone who had experienced such a night patrol himself. For anyone interested in the human experience of the Second World War in North Africa, this is essential reading.'

JAMES HOLLAND, Historian, author and TV Presenter

'When a man has been a soldier and seen action, he writes of war with true understanding, and with authority. When that man writes with wit, elegance and imagination, as Fred Majdalany does in *Patrol*, he produces a military masterpiece.'

ALAN MALLINSON

PATROL

Fred Majdalany

IMPERIAL WAR MUSEUMS

First published in Great Britain in 1953

First published in this format in 2020 by
IWM, Lambeth Road, London SE1 6HZ
iwm.org.uk

ISBN 978-1-912423-15-6

A catalogue record for this book is available from the
British Library.

Printed and bound in Great Britain by Clays Ltd, Elcograf S.p.A

Every effort has been made to contact all copyright holders.
The publishers will be glad to make good in future editions
any error or omissions brought to their attention.

Cover illustration by Bill Bragg
Design by Clare Skeats

About the Author

Fred Majdalany (1913–1967)

FRED MAJDALANY was the son of a Manchester-based Lebanese family. Born Fareed, he insisted on being known as Fred. He was also known as 'Maj'. He was born in Manchester and worked as a journalist and theatre publicist pre-war. Aged 24 he was appointed Dramatic Critic of the *Sunday Referee*, a post he held until the paper was bought by the *Sunday Chronicle* in 1939.

Majdalany volunteered in September 1939 and was commissioned into the 2nd Battalion, Lancashire Fusiliers in 1940. He served in North Africa and Italy. Majdalany was wounded at the Battle of Medjez-el-Bab and returned to the battalion five weeks later with the rank of captain, later promoted to major, and commanded a company. His unit landed at Taranto in September 1943, where he was awarded the Military Cross during the Italian campaign. In 1944 he became second in command of his battalion. In October of that year he was flown home to become an instructor at an officer cadet training unit, which he later commanded, until demobilisation in November 1945.

Majdalany resumed his career as a journalist post-war, writing for the *Daily Mail* and *Time and Tide*. He also worked for the BBC, working on historical scripts for radio and television. His first book publication was a novel of the Cassino campaign published as *The Monastery* in 1945. He published a number of good military histories (including *Cassino: Portrait of a Battle*) which were well received at the time, and continue to be highly thought of. Majdalany's hobbies included early railway prints and vintage motor cars. He suffered a stroke in 1957 and died ten years later, when the specialist commented 'the war killed him'.

Introduction

One of the literary legacies of the First World War was a proliferation of war novels, with an explosion of the genre in the late 1920s. Erich Maria Remarque's *All Quiet on the Western Front* was a bestseller and was made into a Hollywood film in 1930. In the same year, Siegfried Sassoon's *Memoirs of an Infantry Officer* sold 24,000 copies. Generations of school children have grown up on a diet of Wilfred Owen's poetry and the novels of Sassoon. Yet the novels of the Second World War – or certainly those written by individuals who had first-hand front line experience of that war – are often forgotten.

Patrol was a bestseller when it was first published in 1953. Written by the journalist, military historian and novelist Fred Majdalany, the novel displays Majdalany's skill as a writer and the lightness of touch that makes both his fiction and non-fiction extremely readable. *Patrol* depicts the tale of Major Tim Sheldon, for which read Major Fred Majdalany, and his wartime experiences in North Africa. In particular, it tells the story of his journey as a Charlie Company commander, encompassing occurrences such as his time in hospital when wounded, and exploring how central his wartime experiences have been to his life thus far. Yet the real heart of this short, intimate novel concerns Sheldon's command of a night patrol – more of which later.

In regards to the historical context of the work, the North African campaign it depicts is largely remembered today for the Battle of El Alamein, but British and Commonwealth armed forces had been in action there since 1940. Initially, they fought successfully against the Italian army, but when the Axis forces were strengthened with the Afrika Korps – commanded by General Rommel – they proved unstoppable. After Rommel overextended his supply lines, General Montgomery and the Eighth Army finally defeated the combined German and Italian armies at Alamein in November 1942. Operation 'Torch' took place on 8 November 1942. Here a combined Anglo-

American force landed on the coast of Morocco and Algiers (which were under Vichy French control). This advancing force, in conjunction with the Eighth Army from the east, culminated in the capitulation of the German-Italian armies at Tunis the following May.

The fictional battalion of the novel is based on the 2nd Battalion, Lancashire Fusiliers, in which Majdalany served (he also served in Italy). This battalion was part of the Eastern Task Force landing near Algiers, and was one of the infantry battalions of 78th Division in First Army, commanded by General Anderson. The First Army suffered 23,000 casualties during the seven month campaign. Meanwhile, the division itself suffered more than 4,000 casualties, but was instrumental in the capture of Tunis. The intricacies of this Army hierarchy and divisional organisation come out quite clearly in the novel. Infantry battalions such as Sheldon's bore the brunt of the fighting in battles across all the theatres during the Second World War. Majdalany writes:

> At the Battalion you came to the war. Those other places were the war too, but not in the same way. London, Algiers, Army, Corps, Division, Brigade – the long chain of diminishing head offices – all had to be in order that the Battalion might be. To have a spear-point you had to have a spear; though at times it did seem to take an awful lot of shaft to support very little point; but that was a prejudiced notion usually confined to those who chanced to be attached to the point rather than the shaft.

The battalion is constantly in action with little respite; casualties catalyse the regular arrival of reinforcements. Within an infantry battalion, there were usually four companies and a headquarters company. This was broken down into three platoons of 36 men in each company, accumulating to 108 men in total. However the reality in Charlie Company is that there are only 62 men, including four reinforcements. Thus, as Sheldon points out to his newly arrived subaltern, Percy Brooks, straight out from an Officer Cadet

Training Unit, there are 'Two platoons of twenty-one men each plus a commander. I keep the rest here at Company Headquarters, where they are laughingly known as the mobile reserve'. This relentless action and lack of adequate reinforcements mean that Sheldon and others in his battalion are close to battle exhaustion at the novel's opening. Majdalany outlines the Medical Officer's concerns:

> *Now, in a few months of bitter North African winter, he had watched this proud, confident force reduced by continuous action and heavy casualties to a condition in which it was hardly recognisable: a depleted force of reinforcements held together by an over-worked core of veterans, many of whom had had just about all they could stand. What Doc was agitating for – so far without success – was recognition of battle exhaustion as an illness, and authority as a doctor to use his discretion in evacuating men suffering from it. The authorities, though there was some sympathy with the idea, were afraid to commit themselves, Psychiatrists had become the latest fad. There were plenty of them scattered about the base hospitals and convalescent centres to deal with men after they had finally collapsed. But it was still a bit too revolutionary to make it possible for men to be sent back before they collapsed – and so save them to be of further use. Once you let the idea get about that battle fatigue, or whatever you liked to call it, was an illness – why, there was no knowing where it might not lead. So reasoned Authority, sympathetic but anxious to change the subject.*

It is worth remembering – and again the author makes this clear – that these officers, particularly Sheldon, were very young by peace-time standards; a major commanding an infantry company would usually be in his thirties. At twenty-four years of age, Sheldon is only two years older than the fresh-faced subaltern, yet after a number of months in action he states, 'I feel like his grandfather'. The stress of battle ages these young men considerably. This is epitomised by the arc of the lieutenant colonel of the battalion: having taken over command temporarily aged twenty-seven, his once fair hair has turned grey in a mere three and a half months. Indeed through the first half of the novel, which focuses on Sheldon's time 'Being Wounded' (as he officially thinks of it himself) in Algiers, this relative youth and inexperience is often at the forefront of the reader's mind. We learn of Sheldon's past romantic entanglements ('Julie was a bitch, it was as simple as that'), his brief obsession and dalliance with Sister Murgatroyd, and his frequenting of more than one brothel. One particular scene which may make for uncomfortable reading for modern day readers concerns the dancers of the Oulad Naïl – an eye-opening event for the novel's inexperienced protagonist.

Once this background scene has been set, and Sheldon is back at the battalion following a brief stint in Algiers, undoubtedly the central action of the novel – the one which gives Majdalany's work its title – is the patrol itself. There were a number of differing types of patrol across all theatres, but the one depicted here is for reconnaissance purposes – due to a slightly dubious request from divisional headquarters:

> Just then by the merest chance it happened that White Farm caught his eye. Perhaps it was because the White Fathers of Thibar were in his mind; perhaps because there was a tear in the map near there; perhaps it was because the flag which marked it was drooping and the captain was a tidy young man. Anyway, there it was. A prominent feature on the part of the enemy front opposite the brigade for whom a task was being found. White Farm would do as well as anywhere else. It would do fine.

Differing sizes and types of patrols were generally defined as for reconnaissance, fighting or battle purposes. Reconnaissance patrols, inevitably dependent on theatre, fluctuated between two to seven men (at the furthest extremity: one officer, one NCO, and five other ranks) patrolling to obtain information, and not to engage the enemy. Contrastingly, fighting patrols were normally at platoon level to gain information by actively engaging the enemy. Battle patrols were an even larger force to obtain information about the strength of an enemy attack – and delay it. In *Patrol,* the reconnaissance patrol embodies the climax of the novel and is described as 'a complete microcosm of battle'. The sections describing this action are amazing in their intensity and exploration of feelings of fear and isolation, particularly for Sheldon:

> He stared desperately into the dark trying to force his eyes to see, so that they ached more than ever, and he noticed that he was sweating: the sweat was dripping from his eyebrows on to his glasses, so that he had to wipe them. He sensed that the eyes of men were drilling into the back of his neck, so that it felt prickly. Being lost when you are the leader is the worst thing of all. He hated them because he was lost, and could feel their eyes behind him. He hated them because the whole patrol was unnecessary and silly, and because on a night like this it was utterly impossible to find your way. Rage and despair were welling up inside him so that he thought he must let out a great cry, when his foot crunched and he saw that he had stepped on to the gritty hardness of a track. He loved them then and wanted to cry, but for joy.

In these short few scenes Majdalany brilliantly conveys the magnitude and drama of the patrol as the men make their way across the terrain in the pitch black, gain their objective, and then return, in incredibly visceral and evocative prose.

Once the patrol is completed – at considerable cost to the men who have undertaken it – the flagrant irony of its objective is not lost on the medical officer, who comments bitterly: 'I suppose I'm just a fool civilian. But a lot of these damn patrols strike me as being rather silly. It seems a damned wasteful way of finding out whether a probable enemy strong post is occupied in strength'. This is yet further exacerbated by the Brigadier's comment merely of 'Good Show!' The Doctor concludes: 'What a man!... I think his entire range of expression is covered by "good show" and "bad show". If you told him the second coming of Christ had happened I doubt whether he could manage anything more than a tired "Good show!"'

Perhaps most astutely demonstrating the gulf between the wartime officer and the regular officer is Majdalany's following description:

> They have something, the regulars. Not of course, the boneheads who fetch up running reinforcements; or harmlessly in charge of army schools which others run. Not the cosy majors who potter about regimental depots teaching new officers table manners. Not the fourth-raters who use a staff captain's armlet as an excuse for waspish display of minor power. Not those, but the ones who emerge in war: when no one minds your being too young as it's only dying you've got to do, and they can always pull you down in rank afterwards. But, Jesus! they can drive you mad sometimes, those regulars; with their mixture of conservatism and gullibility. If the Brigadier says the comedy is funny then funny it is, don't dare say you thought it terrible. No such thing as not caring to hunt: hunting is correct – you must hunt. And their wives! Those parched numbers from India who love rank more dearly than their husbands. Yet so receptive (these same diehards) to anyone officially classified as an expert. They adore experts. The new craze for psychiatry, for instance. "Trick Cyclists" they were to begin with: till the High Command took them up in a big way. Now it's the thing. "This psychiatry business, old boy... the General's very keen on it." Uncritically accepting something outside their ken they litter the back areas with psychiatrists and are pained because the bad soldier takes advantage of them. But still the best of those regulars have something we can never know.

This encapsulates the real essence of the novel: an inside knowledge of how the army works as an organisation (from a wartime officer's point of view), but incorporating the quintessential relationship of officers and soldiers.

Looking back at his experiences thus far, in the novel Sheldon comments that his life 'began in 1939'. Perhaps this was the case in Majdalany's own life, with war service propelling him to explore alternative avenues, such as his future work as a military historian. He wrote a novel on the Cassino campaign (which he had also experienced), *The Monastery* (1945), as well as a campaign history, *Cassino: Portrait of a Battle* (1957), which continues to be used by historians today. In addition, he wrote histories of the campaigns against the Mau Mau, at El Alamein in North West Europe. After the war, Majdalany's main job was as a journalist and film critic for the *Daily Mail* and *Time and Tide*. He was involved with the PEN club – an international association for writers – where he encountered the novelist and First World War veteran Henry Williamson. It was Williamson who wrote in *The Times* in 1967 to commemorate his dear-departed friend Fred Majdalany: 'the gentle, wise and understanding spirit [he had] will remain with all those lives who were, and remain, the richer for his presence'. The value of this presence has not dissipated with the ravages of time, but continues for a new audience in this reprinted semi-autobiographical novel.

Majdalany's wife Sheila Howarth, stated 'I believe in *Patrol* he was writing his epitaph'. But it has become so much more than that. Rather than solely remembering his legacy, it allows readers an invaluable insight into army life, in what is an almost timeless fictional depiction of an officer's experience during the Second World War.

Alan Jeffreys
2020

ONE

TEN O'CLOCK in the morning, a Monday in the middle of the war. The grey middle when nobody is winning and hope is frozen. Early 1943, but it might have been any other year in the middle of any other war. For the middle winters of war are always the same: grey, timeless, nobody winning.

In a club in St. James's Street, London, an old man stiffly lowered the *Daily Telegraph* he was reading and leaned towards the next chair. A faded spark of aggression struggled fleetingly with the senile glaze of his eyes.

'Why don't they get on?' the old man said. 'What are they waiting for? Why don't they get on?'

The communiqué from Algiers said: 'Nothing to report. Patrol activity.' It had said the same for many mornings.

In Algiers the staff of Allied Forces Headquarters – which seemed now to fill half the town – sat in their offices in the requisitioned hotels and houses and office buildings, attending to their morning mail. As they dealt with documents concerning such diverse matters as gun parts, venereal disease statistics, harbour installations, personnel appointments, special clothing for docks operating companies, summer underwear for nursing personnel, modifications to anti-tank mine fuses, psychiatric treatment at certain base hospitals, faulty ammunition, discipline, boots, and troop movement (to mention a tiny fraction of what lay before them) they grumbled about the weather and chattered pleasantly about their social life. About local families with whom they had become friendly; of the headway or otherwise being made with this or that young woman; of places they had found where you could get something tolerable to eat; of how boring they were beginning to find Algiers. As they slit open the endless buff envelopes and passed the contents, with a scrawl in the margin, to someone else to worry about, many of the male staff officers made dates with the female staff officers, who were now arriving in considerable numbers.

It was all very chummy and unhurried and metropolitan: and remote from the war. Bureaucracy-sur-mer. Whitehall flavoured with garlic and charcoal, combining business and pleasure in a new kind of holiday camp with all found.

Many miles to the east, at Army Headquarters, it happened at ten o'clock in the morning that a colonel in Supply and Transport was saying: 'What it boils down to, old boy, is that for the present men are expendable, tanks aren't. And that's all there is to it.'

To reach Corps Headquarters you had to travel another sixty-odd miles eastwards along that same main road which, if you were patient enough, would bear you all the way from Algiers to Cairo. At Corps the General had been talking irritably about the present defensive role having to continue for the time being. Like everyone else at Corps, the General was tired of being on the defensive. At Corps defence can become very tedious. The General's batman, who always called at the other ranks' cookhouse for a mug of tea at ten o'clock, passed the information on in less formal terms and not quite accurately.

'Accordin' to what the old bleeder was sayin' this mornin',' said the batman, taking a deep gulp of tea, 'we're to go on sittin' on our flamin' arses for the rest of the war.'

At Divisional Headquarters the same sort of office life was proceeding, but it was more compact, more purposeful. So that it seemed more related to the waging of war than the other headquarters. This was a 'glamour' division. It had been doing the work of two ever since the beginning of the campaign. Each of its nine battalions had learned its job in hard little baptismal battles: each had distinguished itself at least once, some of them several times. The reputation of the Division had begun to spread: it was becoming famous for its endurance and its capacity for improvision. Back at home the military academies and their professors were constantly being astonished and even shocked by news of methods which the division – doing the work of two – had developed and employed.

This growing reputation was reflected in the atmosphere at the Division's headquarters – an atmosphere of beaming efficiency. It was like the head office of a prospering young business. The senior officers were younger than the average holders of their appointments. They had the confident aspect of keen young executives who know they work for a good firm. The Division was long overdue for relief. But the additional formations from England, long ago promised, had yet to arrive. You would never, however, be aware of this at Divisional Headquarters.

The headquarters was located, a couple of miles off the main road, in and around a large modern farm owned by a wealthy *colon* who had conveniently fled with his family to Algiers. The farmhouse had been turned into a creditable semblance of an English country club. In the lounge, which was the officers' mess ante-room, you could find the *Tatler,* the *Field,* and *Country Life* laid out alongside the English newspapers. On the walls eight Peter Scott prints did escort duty to photographs of the King, the Queen, and Winston Churchill. Only the presence of the *Dépêche d'Alger* alongside *The Times* served to remind one that this wasn't Surrey.

Sniffing his way round this room like a pernickety housewife was Captain Puttenham-Brown, G3 (Intelligence) and also Mess-President. The Captain, a young Coldstream Officer with a tight, petulant mouth, was in a bad temper. The G2 (Intelligence), his superior, had been away ill for a week. This bad meant a load of extra work. For some days he had been trying to get away to Thibar to pick up some wine which the White Fathers – who made it in their abbey there – had put on one side for him, and now that he had at last got a truck organised and waiting to take him, it looked as though he would never get away. For the cook and the mess sergeant had chosen this of all mornings to have a silly, temperamental quarrel; breakfast had been late and cold; the poor captain had been trying to sort the quarrel out ever since.

Viciously he flicked a few specks of imaginary dust off a side-table with his glove. Savagely he straightened the line of magazines – those damned officers just wouldn't put them back tidily no matter how many notices one pinned up. And now, on top of everything, he found an ash-tray which hadn't yet been emptied from the night before. He screamed, rather than shouted, for the mess sergeant, and as he stood waiting, his handsome, bad-tempered face puckered with annoyance and his foot tapping impatiently, he might (except for the uniform) have been a débutante who has discovered ink on her dress just before leaving for the Palace.

It really was too much (moaned the Captain). As if it wasn't bad enough running Div Intelligence single-handed; trying to get to Thibar for some drinkable wine; exhausting oneself in an effort to run a civilised mess for a collection of officers half of whom had the taste and manners of pigs... The captain had been addressing the sergeant on these lines for some five minutes when an orderly came in and informed him that the General was waiting for him. He looked at his watch and saw that he was late for the ten o'clock conference.

Every morning at this time it was usual for the senior Divisional Intelligence Officer (or, in his absence, Captain Puttenham-Brown) to bring the General's operations map up to date. The latest information from the morning's patrol reports, air reconnaissance, enemy deserters, and local sources was summarised and discussed. The small flags were moved about the large map. New reconnaissance was planned.

'I'm so sorry I'm late, sir,' the Captain said, though his tight little mouth suggested anything but regret. Major-General 'Scratcher' Doyle flashed him a smile of forgiveness.

Doyle was one of the new personality generals, a product of the early Desert campaigns. Not yet forty, he had made himself very popular with this division – chiefly because he dressed badly, was informally breezy in manner, visited battles while they were in progress instead of afterwards, and had an uncanny gift for remembering names. (There is nothing more flattering to a jaded subaltern than to be hailed warmly as Bill by the Divisional Commander.) His nickname, Scratcher, came from a habit of his when lost in thought. He would stand – one leg curled round the other – with one hand cupping his chin, the other scratching his buttocks. One of his more observant officers insisted that the frequency with which the General went through these particular motions had more than doubled since he had discovered what his officers called him and why.

Perhaps his greatest gift was his ability to give unpleasant orders in such a way that he appeared actually to be doing their recipients a favour. Only the day before, for instance, his three brigadiers had been speaking as plainly as they dared about the exhaustion of their battalions. The mounting casualties, the lack of reinforcements, the continuous front line operating since the beginning of the campaign – could not some means be found to relieve units in turn, if only so that they could have a week away from the front? The length of continuous operational duty was abnormal, the wastage of men enormous; the old hands were having to bear an ever-increasing strain. On these lines the brigadiers had said their say.

Quickly the General made it clear that none was more aware than himself of the burden the front line troops were being asked to bear – and were bearing so splendidly. Within a very short time he had persuaded the brigadiers that the present defensive role was the next best thing to a holiday: that it surely wasn't much to ask seasoned infantrymen to do some patrolling too. It was *so* important, he told them earnestly, that, just because one was in defence, one didn't get defence-minded. One must hit and hit and hit – even when the front was static. He was sure their chaps – such *good* chaps – would understand if the position were put to them *frankly*.

So the brigadiers went away and passed on to the battalions the bad news that no relief could be expected just yet: but they passed it on without the beguiling charm of the General, so that the battalions failed to be as impressed as the brigadiers had been.

'Look, Putt,' the General said to Captain Puttenham-Brown, scratching at his left buttock pensively, 'The left and centre brigades have plenty on their plate, but what about the right brigade? Is there anywhere we haven't covered lately? I think we ought to start probing a little deeper.'

The Captain's truck was waiting to take him to Thibar for the wine. The crisis in the mess cookhouse had prevented him from giving the morning patrol reports more than a hurried glance. Once the General got going on these patrol tasks he was liable to fuss and fiddle for hours. If the Captain was to make peace between the mess sergeant and cook *and* get to Thibar (it might be some days before he could again get a truck) he must think of something quickly.

'Yes, sir,' he said, scanning the big wall map desperately. 'Yes, sir,' he said again, playing for time.

Just then by the merest chance it happened that White Farm caught his eye. Perhaps it was because the White Fathers of Thibar were in his mind; perhaps because there was a tear in the map near there; perhaps it was because the flag which marked it was drooping and the captain was a tidy young man. Anyway, there it was. A prominent feature on the part of the enemy front opposite the brigade for whom a task was being found. White Farm would do as well as anywhere else. It would do fine.

'I think we ought to have a look at White Farm, sir,' the Captain said briskly. 'I've an idea the Panzer Grenadiers have pulled out.'

'White Farm?' repeated the General, continuing to scratch his behind meditatively. 'White Farm, you think?'

'Yes, sir. Air Recce has shown a lot of movement there lately. And there have been tips from prisoners and local sources.'

All this was pure invention. But it was said so quickly and so convincingly that the General never for a moment doubted that deep deductive processes had guided Puttenham-Brown to so confident an appraisal of enemy intent.

'Good,' he said. 'White Farm it is, then.'

'Right, sir. By the way, sir. Remember I told you I had managed to get on to some rather special wine? I suppose it will be all right if I go and collect it today. I've nothing much on. And I have got transport.'

'Yes, of course, Putt. Good stuff, is it? Good. We can certainly do with some. Most of this Algerian is filth.'

'It's the nearest to a decent claret we're likely to find this side of the Mediterranean, sir. The White Fathers make it. At Thibar.'

'Splendid, Putt, splendid!'

It took Puttenham-Brown less than a minute to telephone the brigade concerned, and inform them that the General particularly wished a patrol to be sent to White Farm that night. It took Brigade about the same length of time to pass the order to the battalion that would actually have to do it.

The Captain returned to the mess and delivered a sharp dressing-down to the cook and the mess sergeant, who seemed to have patched up an armistice – based, it so happened, on their joint dislike of Puttenham-Brown. He then went outside and climbed into the cab of the 15-cwt. truck: adjusted his Coldstream cap in the driving mirror, with the quick movements of a woman, sighed deeply, and ordered the driver to proceed to Thibar.

At Brigade – a smaller headquarters in a smaller farm, fifteen miles from the front – the Brigadier walked from the mess to his private Elsan. It was ten o'clock and he relieved himself punctually at that time every morning.

At the Battalion you came to the war. Those other places were the war too, but not in the same way. London, Algiers, Army, Corps, Division, Brigade – the long chain of diminishing head offices – all had to be in order that the Battalion might be. To have a spear-point you had to have a spear; though at times it did seem to take an awful lot of shaft to support very little point; but that was a prejudiced notion usually confined to those who chanced to be attached to the point rather than the shaft.

The Battalion had planted its shape, like a hand, on the formless North African landscape: on forgotten ground that was a forlorn scatter of foothills, undulations, and occasional mountains from which the war had driven the few scraggy sheep and their Arab shepherds who normally scratched a living there. Meagre grass and infrequent patches of scrub were the only vegetation. It was a desolation of bare green, mostly bosomy, but exploding here and there into sharp rock outcrops sometimes small, sometimes mountain high: and the green was patterned only by the rock and by the black paths and tracks worn by men's boots and the skid marks of vehicles.

The Battalion Headquarters crouched in a gully a few yards off a track which linked this wilderness to a main road seven miles distant. Forward from the headquarters, like controlling reins stretched the four man-worn paths leading to the Battalion's four under-strength companies, each tactically arranged on a commanding portion of ground: each one a finger growing from the hand that was the

Battalion. By the selection of these positions the Battalion gave shape, tactical shape, to ground that had no other. The companies, fanned out in a rough semi-circle half a mile or so forward of the headquarters, were sited to make little defensive hedgehogs of men and weapons, and they were co-ordinated one with the next so that together they comprised one large integrated hedgehog, the Battalion.

Because of the familiarity of this pattern, the area had developed a positive identity to the men of the Battalion. Here was where they lived and worked and slept and dreamed. Here was where they had lived for many days and nights. This portion of a formless expanse of space had become for the men a place with as clear an identity as a village. It was a place called 'The Battalion'.

At ten o'clock in the morning, on this Monday in the middle of the war, Major Tim Sheldon, officer commanding Charlie Company of the Battalion, was washing his left foot with immense care.

TWO

SHELDON DIPPED HIS left foot carefully into the washbowl his batman had contrived for him by cutting a petrol can in half. He bathed the foot with a fragment of old towel and luxuriated in the coolness of the water, and even the carbolic smell of the soap was pleasant. He scrubbed particularly between the toes, lingering, and then he withdrew the foot and began to dry it, and drying it was even more sensuously exhilarating. Especially between the toes, he especially relished drying between the toes because it tickled a little. The feet are important to the infantryman, for, in spite of mechanisation, the infantry still does much walking. To Sheldon the washing of tired feet was almost the best thing of all in the day's rituals, better in some ways than the shave: though that was good too when you were living rough. He dried the foot with slow deliberation, enjoying the freshening sensation, drying between the toes and tickling and drying, and then for a few moments he held the dried foot – fresh, carbolic, tingling – high in the cold morning air and contentedly felt the pores breathing it in.

It was as though he had provided himself with a new limb. He pulled on a clean sock and stretched it tight so that there were no wrinkles in it and then he pulled on his boot, pliable and glove-soft with use, and laced it up. Finally he put on the small gaiter that binds the boot to the bottom of the trouser leg. He lit a cigarette, stretched himself: then, pulling off the other boot he prepared to repeat the process.

There were no tents. Even if there had been they could not have been used in forward areas – the ground was too bare: they could not have been concealed from the air, and it was the enemy who at this time was in command of the air. For weeks they have lived in open slit trenches with only their waterproofs to cover them, though a few of these trenches, where the ground was soft enough, had been quarried with some ingenuity into dugouts.

The best of these were to be found in the gully used by the

Battalion Headquarters, for there the ground was less rocky. It had been possible in the gully, which was fairly deep, to scratch quite a way into the forward bank as though you were starting a tunnel, and one or two of these cave-like tunnel entrances had been enlarged to quite an impressive size; but the driving rainstorms which had continued through the winter, caused them usually to be water-logged. In the one which served as command post the Adjutant was talking to Brigade on the field telephone. He spoke in a vibrant, musical manner, which seemed altogether too good for the hardy but inelegant little instrument.

In civil life the Adjutant was a B.B.C. announcer, so his beautifully modulated voice gave a somewhat incongruous weightiness to the tedious but convenient army jargon into which he, like everyone else, had drifted.

'Brigade in a flap, as usual,' the Adjutant said – as gravely as though he were delivering the nine o'clock news.

'What is it this time?' the Colonel asked, looking up from a crossword puzzle.

'Division, for some reason, have suddenly become interested in White Farm.'

'We know all about White Farm.'

'I thought so, too, sir,' the Adjutant said. 'But Division seem to think there's something brewing. They think the Panzer Grenadiers have pulled out from there.'

'It's hardly likely. White Farm was established some time ago to be one of their key positions. I suppose we've got to have a look.'

'Yes, sir. Tonight. A strong patrol.'

'Damn Division!' the Colonel said. 'They would do this on us now. Just when the Brigadier has agreed that we can take it easy for a few nights. He knows I'm having to send the same people out every time. Why the hell can't they get us some more bodies if we've got to keep up this pace?'

'Which company had better do it, sir?'

'It'll have to be Charlie Company. Better ask Tim to come down here. Poor Tim.'

The Adjutant called Charlie Company on the telephone.

'Will you ask Major Sheldon to come to Battalion Headquarters?' The voice was formal and composed, as though he were saying, 'Now, here is an S.O.S. ...'

Sheldon was washing his right foot when he became aware of a presence. Lieutenant Brooks, a new subaltern who had arrived the previous night with a handful of reinforcements, was hovering shyly.

'Oh, hello. It's you. Sit down and tell me about yourself.'

Brooks sat down while Sheldon continued to bathe his foot. Why, Sheldon wondered, did these baby-faced boys invariably try to grow a moustache?

'When did you arrive over here?' Sheldon asked.

'Three weeks ago, sir.'

'Straight from England, I suppose?'

'I'm afraid so, sir.'

'You needn't worry about that. You'll soon get the hang of things.'

'I hope so.'

'You don't know how glad we are to see a new officer. We've been under strength for weeks. What's your name?'

'Brooks, sir.'

'I know. What else?'

'Actually – it's Percy, sir.' He said it diffidently.

'Some of my best friends are called Percy,' Sheldon said, withdrawing his foot from the water and beginning to dry it.

'There are some cigarettes in that haversack, Percy. Help yourself and light one for me, will you?' The Lieutenant did as he was told.

'You'll find this a bit different from England, Percy.'

'Yes, sir, I expect I shall.'

'For one thing I expect they taught you that a company consists of three platoons each of thirty-six men.'

'Yes sir.'

'Well, it doesn't. Not when it has been fighting for some time.'

He pulled on a clean sock and placed his foot carefully into the boot.

11

'This' – Sheldon pointed with his towel – 'is a typical company of infantry. There are exactly sixty-two bodies left in Charlie Company, including the four you brought with you last night. Not the hundred-and-whatever-it-is they told you at your Octu. Of these sixty-two, five are back with the transport at B Echelon and therefore, for all practical purposes, in another war. Which leaves fifty-seven. So I've had to reorganise into two platoons instead of three. Two platoons of twenty-one men each plus a commander. I keep the rest here at Company Headquarters, where they are laughingly known as the mobile reserve.

'This powerful Charlie Company is expected to hold this hill feature and the bump to the right which is known as Scorpion Hill. In addition we are expected from these vast resources to send out patrols pretty well every night.'

'There's one thing, sir. Will the men resent very much the fact that I haven't seen any action before?'

'No. Everyone's got to have a first time. When I joined the Battalion practically everyone but myself had been at Dunkirk, I worried about it at first. But it didn't matter. We need some fresh blood. We're a lot of tired old men, Percy. Bloody tired old men.'

'I gather I take over Fifteen Platoon, sir?'

'Yes. Fifteen. How old are you, Percy?'

'Twenty-two.'

Only two years younger than me, Sheldon thought, yet I feel like his grandfather.

'Don't rush things,' Sheldon said. 'They'll take their time to weigh you up. Just give them a chance to get used to you. You've got some good men and you've got Sergeant Prince, who is the best N.C.O. in the Battalion. Get to know them, and about them. Keep your eyes and ears open. Don't talk too much. Above all, don't fuss them. They loathe a new officer who gets in their hair.'

'Right, sir. Well, sir – if you don't want me for anything else – I'll be getting back to the platoon.'

Sheldon watched him walk away. He'd be all right. The keen young public-schoolboy type. The kind that hero-worship easily and bust themselves for the honour of the house. You could laugh at them. You could be irritated by them. But they won your bloody wars for you. Because they had been bred and conditioned to bust themselves for the house. Boys, admittedly. Childish, innocent, naive, and in need of a captain-of-the-school to hero-worship. But they won your wars for you.

The boy had charm, too, Sheldon thought, and charm is one of the most important things for an officer to have.

The Medical Officer signed the last of a number of sick reports and walked from his dugout along the gully of caves to visit the Colonel. Doc was in many respects an unusual man. He always insisted, for example, that he was a doctor first and a military officer second. One of his idiosyncrasies was to encourage the soldiers to address him as Doctor rather than Sir when they visited him professionally. When they come to me, he was fond of saying, they are all patients, just patients, whether they happen to be privates or brigadiers. A point of view, it should be added, which did not commend itself to many of his superiors in the R.A.M.C.

On one occasion in England Doc took on the might of the Church and won. Though himself a man of impeccable morals, Doc, in his capacity of Battalion Medical Officer, took the realistic view that nothing would ever prevent a proportion of a unit's soldiery from consorting with women when such were available. The important thing, as he saw it, was to accept this and do everything possible to prevent unfortunate consequences. He therefore had painted some gaily illustrated posters which drew attention – in the manner of the strip cartoon – to the few simple hygienic steps which a soldier could take, at virtually no personal inconvenience, both before his amours and after; and to the free facilities provided for the purpose by a human and thoughtful Army. These posters were displayed on the walls of the room in which candidates for sick parade normally waited.

This approach to a difficult subject had provoked the wrath of the Padre, who considered them a direct incitement to sin. The C.O., who was something of a politician, had astutely not interfered, holding that this was a case where the executive could best keep out of it and let the lords spiritual and temporal fight it out themselves. The Padre it was who, in due course, asked to be posted to another unit.

The controversial subject on which Doc had most recently been expressing himself forcefully was battle exhaustion. He had been with the Battalion since the beginning of the war. He was one of the few originals who had survived Dunkirk. He had seen it re-form and grow again into a fine unit. He had grown to regard himself (and to be regarded by them) as a member of the unit rather than an attached officer of the R.A.M.C. So much so that he had more than once turned down the promotion that was contingent upon his ceasing to be a unit medical officer.

Now, in a few months of bitter North African winter, he had watched this proud, confident force reduced by continuous action and heavy casualties to a condition in which it was hardly recognisable: a depleted force of reinforcements held together by an overworked core of veterans, many of whom had had just about all they could stand. What Doc was agitating for – so far without success – was recognition of battle exhaustion as an illness, and authority as a doctor to use his discretion in evacuating men suffering from it. The authorities, though there was some sympathy with the idea, were afraid to commit themselves. Psychiatrists had become the latest fad. There were plenty of them scattered about the base hospitals and convalescent centres to deal with men after they had finally collapsed. But it was still a bit too revolutionary to make it possible for men to be sent back before they collapsed – and so save them to be of further use. Once you let the idea get about that battle fatigue, or whatever you liked to call it, was an illness – why, there was no knowing where it might not lead. So reasoned Authority, sympathetic but anxious to change the subject.

It was this subject which weighed on Doc's mind as he walked the few yards to the C.O.'s dugout.

'Come in, Doc.'

'Hello, Colonel.'

They were close to one another, these two. Lieutenant-Colonel Jimmie Morton was twenty-seven years of age, and when they sailed from England he was still a carefree captain with a pronounced aptitude for cricket and getting himself liked. In their first action the C.O. and second-in-command had both been killed. A week later the senior company commander, who had taken over, was wounded. Jimmie Morton had been told to take command of the Battalion until a suitable replacement could be found. He had held the job ever since. He attributed the fact that they no longer thought him too young to the circumstance that his fair hair had in three and a half months turned quite grey. 'They've just forgotten,' he once said. 'They take one look at me and think I'm Grandpa. With any luck they may soon decide I'm too old and retire me on pension.'

The Doctor, five years his senior, was a prop on whom he had leaned with increasing gratitude in recent weeks. Doc was a wonderful person to have around, sane and solid: a kind of uncle to the whole Battalion. But sometimes those ideas of his ran away with him a bit. Not that they weren't sound. But what chance had a poor bloody battalion commander of changing the whole outlook of the British Army? As the Doctor entered the dugout, frowning, the Colonel wondered what it was going to be this time.

'You look stern, Doc. You haven't by any chance come to give me another damned inoculation?'

'I'm worried. I've had another two cases of – call it nerves. Frankly I'm frightened. They're both good men, otherwise I wouldn't worry about it. If we aren't relieved and given some kind of a rest soon, there's going to be a crack-up.'

'I don't think it's that bad, Doc. There are still enough of the old faithfuls to pull something extra when it's needed. You'll see.'

'I'm not so sure, Colonel. It's the old faithfuls I'm worried about.'

'But what can I do about it, Doc?'

'I thought you might be able to put the position to the Brigadier rather strongly.'

'What good will that do? He knows the position. The other C.O.s have had a go at him, as well as myself. If I go on about it he'll simply decide he was a fool to give me the Battalion in the first place. Then they'll dig up some horror from the back areas – some bastard fresh from England who has never heard a shot fired – and send him here with orders to get tough and pull a shaky unit together. The Brigadier is as hamstrung as I am. Only yesterday he said we could let up on the patrols for a few nights.'

'Yes, I heard that,' Doc said. 'That should help.'

'So what happens?' the Colonel said. 'This morning Brigade come on the line with the news that we've got to do a show tonight, after all. A difficult one, too. By special request of the Divisional Commander. So where the hell are you? It isn't the Brigadier's fault. He's simply got to pass the orders on the same as myself.'

'I suppose you're right.'

'The trouble with these people is they've no idea what patrolling means. It's just a phrase to them. "Active patrolling!" They think it just means a nice walk in the moonlight. Something to keep the men from getting bored.'

'Meanwhile,' the Doctor said, 'I suppose the good men will continue to carry the whole show until they drop – one by one. And I shouldn't be surprised if you're one. You've had more than your share. You and Tim Sheldon.'

The younger man laughed.

'You musn't say things like that in front of the Adjutant. He'll start giving me funny looks.'

'Seriously, though, Colonel. If you can wangle Tim Sheldon on to a course or something that will get him away for a bit, it would be a good idea.'

'Tim's my best officer.'

'I know. But apart from yourself he's seen more fighting than any two of the others. He's had about as much as he can take.'

'We'll have to see. Perhaps a course will turn up. He'd probably refuse to go even if he was offered the chance, if I know Tim. Let's have some tea.'

As Tim Sheldon wandered about his Company area, some of the men with whom he chatted thought he seemed more cheerful than he had been lately. They didn't yet know about the easing up on patrols which had been agreed to by the Brigadier the previous night.

'There's a rumour we're to be relieved, sir.'

'There's always a rumour that we're to be relieved,' Sheldon said.

'Sounds genuine this time, sir,' the corporal insisted. 'One of the Brigade D.R.s had it from a chap who heard an officer at Div. tell one of the quarter blokes he'd heard the – '

'I'll believe it when it happens. Even then I'll have my doubts,' Sheldon said cheerfully. 'There's one bit of news, though, which is genuine. The Brigadier is letting us lay off patrols for a night or two, so we can catch up on our beauty sleep.'

'Sentries too sir?' grinned a soldier, and it was at that moment that a runner came up with the news that Sheldon's presence was required at Battalion Headquarters.

This was a most ordinary message, one which he was always receiving, yet for some reason for which he couldn't account Sheldon's heart froze and he suddenly felt sick.

'Come in, Tim,' the Colonel said. 'Sit down. Have a cigarette.'

'Hello, sir.'

'I'm sorry, Tim,' – the Colonel spoke quickly as if to get the bad news over – 'I've got to ask you to do a patrol tonight after all.'

'Tonight?'

'Yes. For some reason Division have suddenly become excited about White Farm. The Intelligence boys think the Boche have pulled out of there.'

'Whenever Div. Intelligence think the Boche have pulled out of anywhere it invariably means they've shoved a lot more people in,' Sheldon said.

'I know, Tim. But the Div. Commander wants this thing done and – well – there it is.'

Quite suddenly there was a series of shrill whines. Aircraft swooping into a dive. Within seconds the pom-pom-pom of cannon-shells, the clatter of machine guns, the whine and shudder of three planes diving in succession, and then the grating, tearing roar as throttles were flung wide for the getaway. Seconds it took, seconds only, and soon the roar diminished to a hum and then to silence.

For some time they continued to sit quite still, staring disinterestedly to their front: the Colonel, the Adjutant, the Doctor, and Sheldon. They sat continuing to stare, controlling the deep relief that fought, like captive breath, to burst through their breasts. The Doctor broke the spell. He was sitting near the entrance and had seen the aircraft dive.

'Abel Company,' he told them.

'Get Abel Company,' the Adjutant told the telephone operator. 'Hello Abel. Anybody hurt? Oh. Right. I'll warn the M.O.' He might have been breaking into the Light Programme to make a grave special announcement.

'Two casualties, sir,' the Adjutant said. 'One a scratch, the other bad. In the arm. Two of the reinforcements who came up last night.'

'Lucky devils,' Sheldon muttered. The Doctor shot him a quick glance, and on the way intercepted the eye of the Colonel. They were too seasoned in the intimacy of fear to pretend with one another, these four.

'Those bloody things petrify me more than anything else,' the Colonel said.

'I'd rather have even those things than mortaring,' the Adjutant said.

'The whole damned lot terrify me,' the Doctor said. 'Well, I'd better go and get my place ready for those two men.'

Sheldon said nothing.

'I'll organise a drink,' the Adjutant said.

'Now then, Tim. About this blasted patrol,' the Colonel said, speaking with a forced jauntiness, 'who d'you think you'll send?'

'I shall be going myself, Colonel.'

'You're the company commander. You shouldn't be going on patrols. You're more valuable doing your proper job.'

'There's no one else.'

'Ainsworth?'

'He was out last night and also two nights ago. I can't send the new subaltern. It wouldn't be fair on the men who had to go with him.'

'It's damned difficult, I admit,' the Colonel said scratching his head. 'I ought to forbid you to go. But I know how awkward it is when we're so short of officers. But it isn't your job to go. Your job is to command a company and that's a full-time occupation: you ought to send Ainsworth. You could explain the position.'

'No, sir. I can't ask old Ainsworth to go out again. Does it have to be tonight?'

'Yes, Tim. Look, I'll have to leave the decision as to who goes to you. According to the book I should order you not to go yourself. But this bloody war gets less and less like the book. I'm sorry, Tim.'

The Adjutant brought some whisky and they drank for a while, but none of them seemed to have anything to say. They were too close to one another to need to try, and after drinking in silence Sheldon merely said quietly that he'd better be going, and left to walk the six hundred yards back to his company.

When he got back he sat down and made out a list of seventeen men whom he regarded as the most reliable ones left in his company. This he sent to the Sergeant-Major with an instruction that they parade, together with Sergeant Prince and the Sergeant-Major himself, at one – as soon as they had finished their meal.

His batman, Perks, handed him his own lunch which consisted of a sausage compressed between two thick slices of bread. It was one of the new tinned sausages that were coming from America – soya links they were called on the tins – and they tasted curiously like rubber, but Sheldon ate his sandwich mechanically without noticing how it tasted. As he ate he felt welling up inside him a helpless rage against the lords of Intelligence who were making it necessary for him to go out that night. How sick he was of the great Intelligence myth with its smug talk about the Big Picture, and its precious Jigsaw Puzzles of evidence. The smooth confidence – so often proved wrong – that this place was weakly held, that place had been evacuated! 'Div are interested in White Farm.' It sounded so impressive. All it meant was that some silly little bastard who hadn't justified his existence lately had said 'Let's have a look at White Farm!' probably meaning somewhere quite different. They put on their big act, those

Intelligence people, of being so bloody knowing. And the generals gaped with admiration and believed everything they said.

That's what it was. Some little shit had looked at an air photo he couldn't understand and seeing some squiggle – probably caused by a fly walking across the film while it was being developed – had decided that it portended vast troop movements. Obviously an offensive was being teed up! If they had to come on these patrols themselves once in a while they wouldn't be so damn free with their brilliant psychic theories about enemy plans.

Sheldon finished his sandwich and his tea and walked over to where the Sergeant-Major had already assembled the men – the Sergeant and the seventeen dependables.

'Sit down and smoke,' Sheldon told them. 'The holiday is over before it has started. We've got to do a patrol tonight after all.

'It's the same old story,' he said, forcing a weak smile. 'When there's an important job we get it. It seems Division want to know what's going on at White Farm. They think the Boche have pulled out. It's terribly important that they have accurate information as soon as possible. You know how it is. These scraps of information seem very small and unimportant to us up here. But by the time they've been passed back from all along the front there's a whole heap of them, and the Intelligence boys can piece them together into a sort of huge jigsaw puzzle that really tells them something.'

(How he loathed this idiotic sales-talk he had given them so often. They couldn't any longer believe a word of it! Yet their pretence of taking it seriously was as convincing as his performance while delivering it.)

'When it's a difficult one the Battalion gets it. If it's impossible Charlie Company has to do it.'

(The same awful joke every time. But what the hell else could you say? They didn't smile. And he didn't blame them.)

'I shall lead the patrol myself with Sergeant Prince as second-in-command. I want five volunteers from you people.'

There was a pause. No one spoke. No one smiled or moved. Then casually, almost indifferently, seventeen hands went up together as if on a secret signal. It was curiously moving, and Sheldon was momentarily struck by the panicky thought that he was going to burst into tears. Why the hell *should* they volunteer? They wouldn't get paid any extra. They would have nothing to show for it afterwards. Nothing to show that they were any different from the soldiers who drove trucks in Algiers and lived in comfortable billets. These men were the veterans of his company, the ones who had borne the brunt of every action. They had earned months of rest, yet it hadn't been possible to arrange for them to have even one day away from the front all winter. He felt a surge of emotion. Why *should* they volunteer?

'Thanks,' he said. 'Question now is which five. Fall out anyone who went out last night.' That brought the number down to eleven. 'And the night before?' The entire eleven fell out, and for the first time since the start of the parade there was a laugh. 'Those eleven over here again. I know. We'll make it a bachelor party tonight. Fall out the married men – they've enough troubles anyway.' That left him with five, the number he wanted.

'Go off now, you five, and get all the rest you can. This one's a long job. It will take most of the night. We'll go out soon after dusk, which will be about eighteen-fifteen hours. I'll brief the patrol here at sixteen-thirty. Teas will be at seventeen-hundred, Sergeant-Major. Extra rations for the men on patrol. Make sure you get some sleep too, Sergeant Prince. If there are any questions ask them now. I shall be in the O.P. this afternoon having a look at the route.'

When they had gone and he could relax again he felt quite weak. He made himself hurry back to his dugout and having collected his binoculars, compass, and map, he set off for the O.P to make his reconnaissance, assuring himself that the walk was all he needed, he would soon be feeling himself again.

THREE

ON THE MAP it was Point 547, but they called it Piecrust because of the escarpment perched, as if as an after-thought, on the topmost ridge. These mountains – topped by curiously shaped escarpments – were a feature of the country, and in this particular region Piecrust was the oddest and most conspicuous, and also the highest available viewpoint. So it had become a part of their lives: visually dominating and functionally important because it was the main artillery observation post for this part of the front, and the Battalion had one there too. It was about a mile to the right of the Battalion, and, because its position was somewhat isolated, a section of armoured cars and a small body of infantry from another unit had the duty of protecting it.

Sheldon walked fast, hoping to reach the summit in about forty-five minutes, but this would be good going as he had to pick his way carefully into dead ground to begin with, to avoid places where you came into view of the enemy, before the mass of Piecrust itself afforded cover. After he had been walking a little while he felt a twinge of pain developing on the ball of his right foot, and he swore as he realised that a blister was developing. A blister, for God's sake! Of all things. Today. He couldn't remember when he had last had one.

He stopped and without unlacing his boot pulled hard at his sock to make certain that it hadn't wrinkled. Then his attention was distracted by eight faint thumps from far off to his front. A gentle chromatic whine mixed with a flutter; the shells burst resoundingly on the slope immediately behind the gully where the Battalion Headquarters was sited. It was strange how impersonal and harmless shells seemed when they were falling on other people – even other people who were your friends. He continued to walk towards Piecrust, and the twinge in his foot was a little better because he had pulled up the sock; but it was still there and he hoped it wouldn't get worse.

For no reason he thought of Brooks the new subaltern being only two years younger than himself; and yet he felt so much older. What strange tricks war played with time. Because you live so intensely. A gallon of living into a pint pot of time. Like when you're in love. The traditional link between love and war isn't simply a romantic fancy. They do have something fundamental in common. Both love and war inject into living a temporary intensity unequalled by other human experience. The images of a man's life are like photographs which fade as they recede into the past. But the photographs of his love periods and his war periods seem to pass through a special fixing chemical so that their outline and detail remain sharp for ever.

I was *born*, he thought, in 1939 in Colchester: I was educated at Aldershot and Catterick: I am now about a hundred years old, having spent most of my long lifetime in a part of North Africa named 'The Battalion'. That is why I am old enough to be the grandfather of Brooks.

There is the faintest recollection of a previous existence. Sometimes I have a curious vision of a life incorporating a Victorian house in Putney, a school on the Sussex Downs, a widowed mother who died with a smile the day after Mr. Chamberlain returned from Munich, and eighteen months with an advertising agency. But I don't believe any of it really happened. Many people have this occasional feeling of having lived a previous existence. It's quite common. There's a simple explanation which for the moment I forget. I don't believe there's really anything in it. My life began in 1939.

Sheldon sat down and lit a cigarette. Again he pulled hard at his sock. There was no hurry. He had all afternoon to spend in the O.P. contemplating White Farm and memorising the route by which he would reach it that night. No point in hurrying unnecessarily. He removed his forage cap, flopped on to his back, and cleaned his glasses. When the cigarette was half finished he rose and continued to walk. The path now began to wind uphill, and he walked more slowly.

As he plodded towards the geological oddity they called Piecrust he began to get a feeling about this patrol. That it was in some way a climax. It was hard to explain. It wasn't a premonition. (No, definitely not a premonition. He didn't believe in those. The chances of survival in the infantry were a matter of plain mathematics and luck; they needed no assistance from metaphysical sources.) It might be that this patrol was a particularly difficult one: a round journey of eight or nine miles and a dangerous approach to the objective. It might be the unnerving, helpless disappointment of having to go out after the promise of a few nights off. It might be that something deep inside, which helped one to keep going, was finally running out. It might be plain weariness – yet nothing could be quite as simple as that.

Perhaps it was that he disbelieved in the value of this operation. He'd been had before by these divisional hunches about strong points being evacuated. He was stubbornly certain that tonight's effort would serve no useful purpose whatsoever. At a time when their physical and moral stamina had been tried to the limit they were being ordered to investigate an enemy strongpoint that was practically impossible to approach without being seen. Was this what he had been leading up to during the hundred years of intensified living he had lived since being born in Colchester in 1939?

He began to muse again on the relativity of time in war, and the episodes of this life began to unfold themselves in his mind like a film. On the screen of his weary consciousness the images of the past began to flicker: the images of the phantasmagoric progress by which he had arrived at this ultimate bathos, this final unfulfilment, this climactic negation – the patrol to White Farm...

A wet afternoon which began in the sulphurous catacombs of Liverpool Street Station in London and ended at the garrison town of Colchester. The swift and shattering disillusion of the eager volunteer who comes pleading to serve and is pulped in two days into a shivering inferiority complex. Quick march, left right, left right, wot the 'ell's wrong with you there, third from the left, rear rank, you I mean, yes you with the big 'ead. Quick march, left right, get your 'air cut. And when I says double I means double. Wot we're goin' on with now is lesson one, Characteristics of the Bren – get

your 'air cut. Wot we're goin' on with now is lesson two, 'Oldin'
and Aimin', get your 'air cut. Wot we're goin' on with now is lesson
three, Loading' and Firin', – get your 'air cut. Chapped hands,
blue with cold, aching from fumbling collision with unyielding gun
mechanism in a despairing anguish to please the god with three
stripes. Quick march, left right, get your 'air cut.

Octu. Back to a glossier egg to be hatched again, and still it hurt;
and the thing that hurt most was being bad at it. That is perhaps
the worst humiliation of all: to be trying so hard, so very hard to do
something for which you are unsuited and to be no good. (Women
are no help, they just say it's doing you a world of good, ha-ha,
they've never seen you looking better, ha-ha.)

Commissioned. The first sly peepings of incipient confidence.
Regimental depot packed to bursting with lots like you arriving
weekly with oh-so-new service dress, brown gloves, and little stick.
New boy again. (No, sir, I'm afraid I don't play bridge. No, sir. I'm
afraid I don't hunt. No, sir, I'm afraid I don't shoot. No, sir, I'm
afraid...)

The Battalion was the turning point: the beginning, really. It was
just back from Dunkirk. The embarrassment of being the only one
who hadn't been at Dunkirk was difficult. But for the first time you
belonged. You were junior and desperately aware of it, and this was
a very Regular battalion. But for the first time you were accepted.
You belonged somewhere. Imperceptibly it became easier. You were
beginning to cope. Hard to say when you were first aware of this. It
happened. You were no longer quite so bad at it. It was still strange,
unreal. But there was now the boost to the vanity of being passable
at something outrageously not for you.

The invasion summer was wildest fantasy. On a clifftop on the
south coast you patiently awaited the descent from the skies of
swarms of bullet-headed Huns armed with machine guns. The only
terror was to get to your section posts in time to wake up the sentries
before the C.O. reached them on his rounds. (It was impossible to
make a man from Dunkirk take the invasion of England seriously.)
So worrying was it cycling up and down the clifftop waking up
sentries you hardly noticed the streaks doodled in the sky, the remote

scream of planes invisibly high: it was not till later you heard they related to something that became known as the Battle of Britain.

There was something else too. Some anti-personnel mines came, fifty of them. A new type. They said only the sappers must handle them. Next day three came, a subaltern, a corporal, and a sapper. Off they went with the mines and later that afternoon you went along to see how they were getting on, as they were putting them on your sector. They'd nearly finished, and you chatted for a while and told the officer to come for a drink when he'd finished, then you walked away. You had gone less than a hundred yards when there was a flat explosion not much louder than a bunting balloon. You hurried back.

The torso of the officer, very white and clean lay in the cratered minefield. No head, no legs, the bottom of the so-white stomach ripped like paper. His badges of rank survived unspoiled to identify him. One of the others – couldn't tell which – was yards away, strung up on the barbed wire in an attitude of inverted crucifixion. His legs tidily together, his feet placed like a dancer taking off on a pirouette – but upside-down and the arms so neatly outstretched. The appalling *neatness* of violent death. Your first taste.

The third man had vanished completely. He just wasn't there.

Long months of training, courses, and exercises, huge chaotic exercises which went on for days at a time and no one ever knew what was happening. The hardening marches and the battle schools. Then to Scotland for combined operations on Loch Fyne. A fortnight aboard a training ship: luxurious Navy food, gin at threepence a nip, learning to climb up and down rope ladders. Suppose all that happened, too, though it is hard to be quite certain; it has so little bearing on *this*.

All that time, too, there was Julie. How long ago Julie seemed. Sheldon smiled. He couldn't even recollect her face. Yet she had been important in those years. Since the early days of the war there had been Julie, and vaguely he had drifted into a belief that there was an understanding – that's the word, isn't it, understanding? Very adolescent, he now realised. She worked in London. He always took her out on leave. Between, he built her up in his imagination. Every leave he proposed: every leave she gently headed him off. Never for a moment did he doubt that Julie was the girl whose photograph would eventually travel abroad in his breast pocket. That Julie was the one who would sit at home and miss a heartbeat whenever a telegraph boy approached the house. In the periods of separation between leaves his imagination worked on her, building her up, and the few hours together during a seven-day leave were insufficient to dismantle the goddess and expose the reality. The reality (now it could be breathed) was disturbing: Julie was a bitch, it was as simple as that.

For eighteen months she had lived with that Canadian Colonel who worked late, four nights a week, at Canada House – so Julie could have other friends and lead you up the garden path all that time. Julie let you take her out and kept you warm for the most basic of all reasons. Julie was always hungry and liked to eat well, you fed her well – that was all there was to it, the little bitch. It took a long time to face such ordinary facts, but there's nothing like a forced march in the Highlands to sweat things out in every way and suddenly, without you noticing it particularly, it was all right. There has to be a Julie or two in every man's life – but, oh, the time wasted, the opportunities missed. How one envies extroverts like Martindale. Martindale would be having a drink with you. Then suddenly he'd excuse himself and follow a girl out of the bar, a girl he'd never seen before. He'd hire a cab for fifteen minutes and be back with you almost before you'd finished the drink. (He'd do this as easily in Bournemouth or Cairo.) Damn you, Julie!

So the education ended, and one day not long afterwards they said in the middle of the Atlantic that now you could be told that North Africa was where you were going...

Sheldon was panting a little now, for he had started to climb the steep rocky path which wound to the top of Piecrust. He could see the Battalion positions below and behind him. They were being shelled again, but not Charlie Company as far as he could see. A thought struck him, and he smiled. How very young he must have been right up to the end of Julie, as young as Brooks the new subaltern!

A louder whine with a buzz to it, and four shells burst below along the path where he had been walking ten minutes before. Instinctively he made for the nearest hollow and pressed into it. Damn their eyes, they were starting to shell Piecrust. The shells began to come over. They came fast and in groups of eight but they landed comfortably below where he was. But you never knew when they were going to lift: or one would drop short. He moved to a crevice where he could rest until the shelling stopped. He was tense with fear now. He'd got bad at shelling. Thank God there was no one about to see. His fear brought on another wave of bitterness about the patrol. The shells continued to burst close, but safely below, exploding with tremendous crashes which reverberated along the valley. If he didn't get up now he never would. He made a great effort and resumed the climb, and was glad when he saw some soldiers in the distance, because he would have to put on an act of not minding the shells and this would help him to keep control over his nerves. He must stop thinking about the damned shells, that was all. But his mind could only dwell on the vivid past, on the images of remembrance that had been through the indelible fixing process. Again he had the oppressive sense of impending climax. The summit of the hill, looming now close above him, seemed to become the symbol of that climax, for in a short while he would be able to see from it the dreaded objective, White Farm. So he drove himself forward up the hard, angled mountain track and tried to avoid thinking about the shells which were still coming over, and again his mind involuntarily slipped back. The England part had been the youth, the Africa part the manhood...

The first time you're shot at. It can't happen to you. Ordinary men don't get shot at. Not a bit what you expected. What did you expect? Hard to say. But not that. Something more dramatic, perhaps. Something more important. But it wasn't like that at all. You were walking down a road strung out in a long single file. There was a moon. A stream of red pours prettily across your front some way ahead – there is another company strung out ahead of yours. You happen to be wiping your glasses on which sweat drips from under your tin hat. Blasted glasses. Do people who don't wear them know what the rest suffer? A voice says casually, 'Leading company must have run into something.' It has happened at last. Ever since Colchester you have wondered about it, wondered how you would be. There was the usual fear of fear. Everyone has that before the first time. Now, it is actually happening, and you don't seem to be afraid. Nothing for you to do yet. The leading company, deploying in routine advance-guard fashion, will discover whether this is a small post or something more. You've done this advance-guard stuff dozens of times on training – funny to be doing it with a real enemy. Leading company's Brens opening up now. They sound slower than the enemy gun, the one that is throwing the pretty red tracer. I suppose the other side's guns always sound faster and fiercer. Still nothing for you to do. There may be soon if the trouble is too big for the leading company to handle alone. Just tell your lot to stay under cover in the ditch and keep a good look-out all round. That's all – too easy. May as well stroll up the road towards red tracer and find out what is happening. There may be orders. How peaceful it all is. You notice the different noises the bullets make. Sometimes 'whee-ee-ee', sometimes 'psst'. In books it used to be 'ping'. But they do not seem to 'ping'. The C.O. is leaning against a wall at the side of the road. He seems disinterested. He is waiting for a signal from the leading company, he wants to get on. He doesn't think it is more than an outpost: a section at the most, he thinks. The main enemy positions are farther on by the river, the main positions which we are probing forward to locate, for we are leading the advance to contact, as they impressively call it. We are the tip of the spear-point of the whole army at this moment. (How odd! Us!) The C.O. says better have your company ready to go round by the left if the opposition turns out to be stronger.

You walk back down the road and give the necessary orders, orders that are easy and almost automatic. There seems to be a lot of time. Much more time to do what you have to do than there used to be on exercises. On exercises you always had senior officers and umpires fussing round trying to catch you out, flustering you, telling you to get a move on. The real thing is so much easier. No one excited. Lots of time. Having prepared your company for action if required, you stroll back to where the C.O. is. Then something scorches past your face. You duck – long after it has passed because your untrained reflexes are still slow, but you duck all right and you feel a spasm of fright. Your voice is a long way off. Tracer all of a sudden seems less pretty. But the fright passes almost immediately as you are still fresh physically. It has been almost stimulating. Your voice has returned. Already you feel tough and seasoned. There's nothing to it after all!

Not many days later you know all the sounds and your ducking is instinctive and precise. You know when to duck and when not to, exactly. But your heart tends to thump whenever anything comes your way, because now you know all about it. As soon as your heart thumps all the time you can call yourself a veteran. The first time you're shot at is the only time you feel brave. Because you don't know. (It did turn out to be an outpost – four men and a machine gun – they left hurriedly when the leading company opened up on them.)

A nameless pimple in the middle of nowhere. How many of those there have been. How difficult they would be to find after the war. A barren hump of unmemorable ground. It became important to a few human beings for a few hours of a November afternoon. Some of them lay on and about it in holes: some others wanted it. It wouldn't matter a great deal in the eternity of time who any of them were. Nor, in the larger pattern of conflict, why the hill was to desirable. This was one of the smaller battles. The ones that don't get into the newspapers. Little battles whose only historians are the casualty telegrams. We were the ones who had the hill. About a hundred of them tried to push us off it late one afternoon. It was only a small battle, no good for the films. They came closer and closer, and we watched them go through motions we had so often practised ourselves. Fire and movement: short section rushes from cover to cover while the machine guns tried to keep us quiet. A steady pounding from mortars – supporting them from well-hidden positions to their rear – the mortar bombs dropping all over our hill in the unpredictable vague way they do, which is why they are terrifying. (Not like calibrated, well-brought-up shells which go precisely where they are directed and stay on a spot until the gunner makes a switch.) But our own stuff was pouring back on them, and the power of the weapons was impressive and exhilarating. But still they came closer, working round the flanks, using the curve of the ground cunningly. Closer, despite their casualties, and they were very close indeed.

They came into the final assault shouting. Open up with all you've got. They falter. Some fall. They start again led by a tall officer. Keep firing, damn you, keep firing. The climax. The sudden shedding of the last veil of reserve. Fear is the goad. Fear. Yell, man, yell and get after them. Shout. Shout anything. Fix bayonets and chase them back where they came from. The order to fix bayonets is strangely heartening, a sublimation of fright; you give the order, scramble out of your hole, and lead the counter-charge. Weakened by losses and tiredness, they hesitate and begin to run. Get after them yelling, yelling, yelling. Hysterical yells, gibberish. Temporarily without fear, temporarily inexhaustible, lead your lot running, firing, shouting. Down the slope yelling. Wonder what I yelled. It is easy to lead for a few seconds of battle climax because frightened men long for a positive order and will obey any that is given. So long as you say something definite... anything...

That night, widows in Liverpool, Blackburn, London, and Hull. Jones will lose an eye. They may save Johnson's leg. That was our second battle. But it was our first experience of winning...

Sheldon hadn't much farther to go. He passed a group of soldiers huddled round a tommy cooker, shielding it with their hands to make the water boil faster. Chatting with them was the captain in charge of the armoured cars at the bottom of the hill. The captain, a long bony fellow with a thin foolish face and a handle-bar moustache, greeted Sheldon heartily.

'Come to admire the view, sir?'

'That's right,' Sheldon said.

'On a clear day they say you can see five counties. But we've never had a clear day so we don't know.'

Four shells screeched low over the escarpment.

'They seem active this afternoon,' Sheldon said, lingering unnecessarily because where he was there was good cover.

'Almost offensive,' the captain said, and Sheldon hated him unreasoningly because he seemed unconcerned. 'If you feel like a quick one on the way back I'll be down with my section,' the captain said. 'Drop by if you care to.'

Sheldon thanked him and panted up the last few yards to the observation post, which was on the left of the crest below the escarpment. The actual observation point was a hole that had been scooped out just below the crest, so as not to be visible from the enemy side. To enter it without being seen it was necessary to crawl along twenty yards of approach trench that had been cut to a point well below the crest. Sheldon crawled along it and wormed his way into the observation post, which successive occupants had enlarged to a deep and reasonably roomy hollow. The climb had made him hot, and his glasses were steamed up. He removed and wiped them, lit a cigarette, and took off his right boot to ease his blistered foot.

Then, lying on his stomach, he raised the binoculars to his eyes and turned them on to White Farm, a faint white blur partly sheltered by a wood. Then, lowering the binoculars, he pulled out his compass, map, and notebook. He took a bearing from Piecrust to White Farm and calculated the back bearing; then a bearing from Piecrust to the Battalion. Next he worked out the same bearings on his map and satisfied himself that the results were the same. It was an elaborate precaution he would not normally have taken. But he was leaving nothing to chance: these pre-war French maps they had to use weren't always reliable. Then he took more bearings on the more conspicuous landmarks and noted these. White Farm, he calculated, was a good four miles in a direct line. It would be farther on the ground. The patrol would take most of the hours of darkness. If they ran into trouble it might take longer, and he might have to return by a roundabout route. It would be helpful in that eventuality to have a few bearings up his sleeve from which useful back bearings might be worked out if the return journey became tricky.

His foot had cooled so that he could no longer feel the blister, but when he felt with his fingers it was still there. He replaced the boot without lacing it up. Then he lit another cigarette and settled down again with his binoculars, wriggling on his stomach until he had made himself as comfortable as the hard rock permitted.

He swept the binoculars slowly from right to left, from left to right, then again from right to left. As he did so he remembered his first lesson in observation, given by a freckled, parrot-faced sergeant named Perkins.

'Wot we're goin' on with now,' Sergeant Perkins had begun in the time-honoured way, 'is hobservation. The object of hobservation is to teach you to hobserve c'rectly and systematic. Now you all 'as a pair of eyes in your bloody 'eads – though some of 'em looks a bit on the baggy side this mornin', if I may make so bold as to pass a remark – and some of you probably thinks as 'ow you can hobserve already. Well you're bloody well wrong, if you'll pardon my French, because hobservation – c'rrect hobservation that is to say – is not the same as plain 'aving a dekko, see?'

An area under observation, the good Sergeant continued, must be divided into foreground, middle distance, and background. The observer should begin by scanning the foreground from right to left; continue from left to right across the middle distance; finally sweep from right to left across the background. In this way, the Sergeant explained, the ground would always be thoroughly covered.

After dealing with these and other fundamentals of methodical observation, Sergeant Perkins had gone on to reduce the wonders of nature to a few simple terms.

'Some of you people,' he had said, 'may 'ave picked up in your nature study lessons at college a lot of fancy names. Well forget 'em see? The Army is full of private soldiers who 'aven't been to college. And when a target is being pointed out it is 'ighly essential that every man knows wot you are talkin' about.

'In the army,' he announced portentously, 'there is only three kinds of tree: pine, poplar, and bushy-top. When you are describing a target or a landmark you will never refer to a tree as anything but pine, poplar, or bushy-top.'

They had smiled, but they had remembered. A simple procedure, well planted at the beginning, had been absorbed into instinct, and emerged in a crisis as a support. Sheldon, exhausted by a surfeit of combat, by responsibility, by lack of sleep, proper nourishment, and warmth: a tired spirit driving body and nerves to an effort they were crying to avoid – Sheldon, acting purely by instinct, swept the ground with his binoculars from right to left, left to right, right to left, precisely as Sergeant Perkins had enjoined.

He swept the ground and swept it again, feeling it with his eyes until they hurt, stroking and patting every fold and curve of it, pressing its shape into his consciousness, pressing, pressing hard so that it would be printed unforgettably on his memory. Three months ago he would have regarded such a reconnaissance as an unavoidable nuisance, almost a waste of an afternoon that might have been spent resting. He would have run over the ground a few times with his glasses, taken a few bearings, made some notes, and quickly left. Today he peered at the ground till his eyes ached. And after every sweep his glasses came to rest on the white farmhouse that disappeared into the trees: trying to catch the faintest trace of movement, or some object that would give a clue to what was happening at the farm. But all the time he watched he saw nothing. Not even a puff of dust to indicate that a vehicle might be moving in the vicinity. It was just a white farmhouse, with outbuildings, a farmhouse which disappeared, on one side, into trees. He pondered a long time the best approach to the farm and finally decided the lesser of the evils would be an approach from the right. The trees to the left were an obvious covered approach and would be likely to be well defended. The front was quite open – out of the question. The right was fairly open, but there were the farm buildings when you got close. He would go in from that side considering that that was the side from which the enemy would least expect attack, because of its openness. But it was a toss-up which approach one chose. It was asking for trouble to go to the place at all with less than a company.

The grey clouds burst into a drizzle, but Sheldon, hardly aware of it, continued to stare at White Farm and the ground that led to it, feeling it and pressing it with his eyes, pressing it into his mind…

The Colonel was alone in his dugout when the Medical Officer entered.

'I gather you're letting Tim Sheldon go on patrol tonight,' Doc said.

'The decision was his.'

'You're the C.O. I wish you'd stop him.'

'It's his own decision, Doc.'

'He isn't fit to go. I wish you'd stop him.'

'I can't. If things were normal it would be different. He's been operating with one other officer for three weeks. They've both had a bashing. Ainsworth's tired too: he's been on patrol on two of the last three nights. It was Tim's idea not to ask Ainsworth to go tonight. He insisted.'

'Can't that new man go?'

'No. Brooks has only just arrived. More or less straight from England.'

'He's got to start some time, hasn't he? He looked a good man to me.'

'It isn't him. It's the men that go with him. With the Battalion in its present state we can't risk losing half a dozen of the few good men we've got left through the inexperience of a young officer.'

'I don't understand anything about military matters. I'm just a doctor. And as a doctor I feel bound to say that Tim isn't fit to go out on this show tonight.'

'I wish it wasn't necessary,' the Colonel said wearily. 'But I see Tim's point in going himself.'

'Is this a particularly difficult patrol?' Doc asked.

'Yes, it is rather.'

'Is it a long way, or something?'

'That's one thing. There's barely time to get there and back in darkness.'

'What have they got to do? One takes this damned word patrol so much for granted.'

'In this case they have to check on an Intelligence tip that White Farm has been abandoned. If it's true, then they will merely have a long walk in the night air. If not they're likely to get in a fight, in which case they get to hell out of it as quickly as they can and bring back as complete a report as possible of what they think they got in a fight with.'

'Let's hope that Div are right, then, Colonel.'

'I hope to Christ Div are right.'

The Adjutant poked his head through the entrance.

'The Brigadier is on his way up, sir,' he said. For a moment it seemed as though he were going to add: 'So as we have two or three minutes before the next programme, here is a gramophone record...'

Sheldon took a last hard look at White Farm. Then, stuffing his map and notebook inside the blouse of his battledress, he crawled backwards down the approach trench, swearing as his knees rubbed against the sharp stones which were loosened as his toe-caps slithered over them. When he was clear of the trench he sat down, laced up the boot he had taken off in the O.P., and smoked a cigarette, giving his body a chance to recover from the confinement of the observation hole.

When the cigarette was finished he set off down the hill, and he hadn't been walking long before he could see the armoured cars below in the valley. There was some activity near them, and looking through his binoculars he saw that a stretcher was being loaded onto a Bren carrier that had a red cross painted on its side. Lucky devil, *his* troubles were over! To be wounded was the only mercy left. Except death, of course. But you never thought much about death when it was so available. It would have been unwise to let yourself. Death had to be a forbidden thought. Something which happened to other people. To be wounded was the thing, provided it wasn't too painful. Not in the head or the stomach or the spine or the privates. That reduced the target area a bit, admittedly. Mustn't be too choosey. But it left quite a lot of body. Blessed gunshot, beloved shrapnel, when you choose the right place and do not overdo it!

Sheldon had been wounded quite early in the campaign and he had grown to look back on it with nostalgia as on a well-remembered holiday, an enchanted interlude.

Being wounded was many things: ambulances, being fussed over, emancipation from worry, everyone being kind. It was the brown hospital, baby-blue blankets, the station, the train, the white hospital. Being wounded was Algiers and the fantasy of Leavetown; it was authorised madness, licensed unreality; being wounded was Women. Being wounded was all these things and many beside, but first it was red tracer...

FOUR

RED TRACER IN THE AFTERNOON: red tracer from a tank, the ground bare and open. Why did you choose this time to visit that damnable section on the left? Silly time to be social. No hope of getting back now except on your belly. Get down. Crawl and pray, pray hard. Line of tracer sweeping from right to left. At least you can see tracer, that's something. Line of red peanuts, no, peardrops, sweeping from right to left. Will reach you in two seconds. It passes without hitting. It will sweep back in a moment. Coming now. Keep down. Lower, you fool. Press the body hard into the ground. Coming now. Thin red line, so pretty, scissoring back. Keep praying. Wish you couldn't see it now, wish it was ordinary bullets, at least you can't see them. Here we go. It passes again, don't believe it. Next time for certain. Can't move. Nicely caught in its arc. Hell's scissors. Snip, snip. Fellow probably can't see you. Can't see much from a tank. They just spray and spray and hope for the best. At least that's what you were always told. Not so sure now.

No need to visit that section. Except that it cheers them up when you show your face. This counter-attack is nasty. Never knew ground could be so devoid of dents and hollows, nowhere to go, here it comes, press down, what a big backside, big as a mountain, must be visible miles away. The red lines swinging back: this time for certain, for certain, for... dull ache in your right leg, something firing back at them hard: a clap of thunder. The tank is in flames, black oil smoke, hurry, hurry, hurry, crawl to that ditch at the roadside, quick.

Hot fluid down your leg. Pain. Hot, sticky blood fills the inside of your trousers – feel sleepy. The battle is the consummation, the wounding the orgasm. Strange feeling of relief, indescribable relief for some reason. In a way a sense of fulfilment. The logical climax after all the theories and speculations: the practical worries and anxieties of trying to lead. The final essence of war shorn of the manuals, the pageantry, the science the theory. This is what it was all for.

This is the fulfilment. You don't know till you've been wounded. All over now. Wonderfully over. Oh, hell, hold on.

Another tank coming up the road, you're pinned in the ditch, the tank is coming straight towards you. 'Blood on the tracks.' Damn that silly phrase. A hearty battle-school instructor, the ferocious non-combatant type, gave the title to a lecture. 'Blood on the Tracks'. People foolishly scared of being crushed by tank tracks, pooh-poohed superman. So silly, he said. Only thing to worry about with tanks is their guns. Purely psychological, he said, this fear of tank tracks, no one ever crushed by tank. Like to have you in this ditch now, you bastard, you and your 'Blood on the Tracks'. It is eighty yards away grinding forward steadily. Seventy, sixty, fifty. Hell. Thirty, twenty yards. It has stopped and sprays with its machine gun and pumps shells up the road, but the hypnotic tracks, broad steel teeth, are still. It is edging forward again, it will miss you by a yard if it does not swerve, please God, it's true you can't see much from a tank, why aren't ditches deeper in this damnable country, press down, it is less than ten yards away, it has stopped again, don't they ever run out of ammo, he has been firing continuously, but the wide steel teeth are still, there is a deafening crash stunning the ear drums, a shower of dirt – keep your eyes closed and pray, what was it? don't move, no sensation, blackout... The tank is in flames, hurray, hurray, the tank was caught fair and square, it burns quicker than the other, it's hot as hell, smell of burning oil, get out quick, get back. That's better, rest here for a bit, damn, that has made your leg hurt more. Over there grey figures running, all across your rear your guns opening up, ripping wide the dusk to rain on the grey figures retreating, they're running away, their attack has failed, they're going back, you can get back now too. Better wait a little though, make certain the counter-attack is beaten off, don't get caught in own fire... Jesus it is a long way. The blood lining the trousers feels cold and crusty, must have been lying there some time, must have passed out. The leg is iron-hard and twice as big. Keep going. Aches more than before. Can't be too bad or wouldn't be able to walk. Voices, must be Baker Company, good old Baker, not far now.

Yes, I'm fine. No, thanks. Fine, thanks. Hello, Doc. A stretcher is the softest bed in the world. Bliss. Blood-lined trouser leg ripped off with a knife. Blood and dirt, the leg is iron-hard and twice as thick, is wavily red-clotted from the knee down. Sweet sickness. No more worry. Tired, so very, very tired...

First it had been ambulances and sleep. He awakened as they put him into one, and as they hoisted him out. He was in a large school hall, with yellow walls, and full of wounded like himself. The stretchers were along the walls pointing out into the middle of the hall, and in the centre there were two operating tables where some of the wounds were examined and re-dressed. The white coated doctors wore steel helmets as an air raid was in progress. This was the Advanced Dressing Station. Tremendous shuddering crashes rocked the building, and one of the doctors was in a temper, saying, what could they expect when they surrounded the place with anti-aircraft guns. Someone handed you a cup of tea, and you noticed that you had a label tied to your tunic. Like an evacuee child. It said your name and unit, the date and nature of your wound, described a G.S., which stood for gun-shot.

He was too tired to notice the air raid. Soon he was asleep, and again he awakened only when they lifted the stretcher into the ambulance and when they took it out. Now he was in a barn lit by a few hurricane lamps, and less like a hospital than the school hall had been. As he could see through a doorway that it was dark, he wondered whether this was the same night or the next. It turned out to be the next. He had slept through a day. Was this the Casualty Clearing Station where the bullet would be removed? No, they said, this was Railhead. They gave him a lot of those new pills – sulphur-something-or-other – for shock or it might be tetanus. Then he was carried aboard a train, an aluminium streamlined affair converted into an ambulance. He slept through most of that journey, too, awakening as usual, though, when the stretcher was lifted out of the tram and carried to an ambulance, oh, God, another ambulance! But it wasn't far this time. Taxi from the station. Soon he was in the Casualty Clearing Station – a civil hospital – this must be a fair-sized town.

Here the stretcher cases and the walking wounded were all taken into a large reception hall, and there he noticed for the first time that there was a German among the walking. A harmless little fellow, he looked. About thirty-five. Shy and embarrassed about the cigarettes his enemies offered him. Not exactly the storm trooper one expected. He'd have looked right in a cloth cap, a watch-chain across his middle, walking a plump wife to the pictures on Saturday night. (It turned out that he was a clerk at a training school which to its surprise and annoyance was flown to North Africa as a stop-gap fighting force early in the campaign: the school had the misfortune to be in southern Italy and could be got to Africa quickly to help out until proper troops could be sent.)

An orderly came in and started to take details from each man, including as always, religion. (They were very particular about that. You must be buried right, if the question arose.) When he came to the German the orderly could not make clear what was wanted. A corporal of the Lancers, one who had given the German a cigarette, took over.

'*Qui est votre religiong?*' demanded the corporal in a loud, clear voice.

The German smiled apologetically.

'*Votre religion. Religiong,*' the corporal persisted. It was no good. He tried a different approach.

'*Vous!*' As he said it it he pointed vigorously at the German. '*Vous avez Catholique?*' On the last word he thumped out the sign of the cross four times with his clenched fist.

'*Catholique?*' he repeated, again making the sign of the cross.

The German shook his head with infinite apology.

'Not R.C.,' the corporal explained to the rest of them, scratching his blond head. He tried again.

'*Vous!*' he began again. '*Vous avez Church de Englong? N'est-ce pas? Ch-our-ch de Eng-long?*' The little German shook his head, and his sadness at being unable to help was touching. The corporal scratched his head and mopped his brow. Then his face lit up.

'*Vous Protestant? Pro-test-ant. PRO-TEST-ANT.*' The man nodded happily. The orderly noted it down and passed on.

They carried you up to a small room and left you for a long time. Then a cheerful doctor came in, followed by orderlies. He pricked you in the arm, and when you woke up you were in the same room and it was still daylight, but you found out after that it was the next day. At the bedside an envelope. On it someone had written 'You may like these as a souvenir'. One lump and a few bits of metal. Disappointingly small. You must have worked off your arrears of sleep, you felt wonderful. You were no longer on a stretcher but in bed. Still dirty, but in bed. Wonderful. It could go on forever. They kept you in there that night and the next morning they carried you downstairs to an ambulance. This time you didn't sleep. You'd at last had your fill. For the first time you began to be a little bored lying in the ambulance with nothing to look at but the brown canvas of the stretcher above you, an empty stretcher with a dried bloodstain showing on the under-side. The road was rough and twisting, and the ambulance rocked a great deal. There was another casualty alongside you but he slept most of the time, his only social contribution to the journey being a frightful smell, so that you were glad when, after two and a half hours, the ambulance at last stopped. When they lifted you out you were in a large clearing.

They carried you over to a group of tents and you saw that men were busy erecting others. The hospital had evidently arrived only a short time before the patients.

For many timeless days and nights being wounded had been ambulances and sleep. Now it was a brown tent.

Do wounds always ache at sundown? His did. He always knew exactly when the sun set because his leg began to throb. Then, almost immediately the planes would arrive for the nightly bombing of the airfield a few miles away. The wound and the bombers were always punctual; they became his calendar.

There were twenty beds along each side of the long brown tent. These were twice as many as there should have been, but tents were short. It meant that the beds were so close that you couldn't even get your arm between yours and the next. On the beds were pale baby-blue blankets, soft as down, and below them crisp white sheets, but the bodies that lay on them were filthy, and some, when they arrived, even kept on their mud-encrusted boots. It was nobody's fault. It was early in the campaign, and to begin with they had used a civil hospital in the town, but it was on the sea front and soon it was hit during one of the daily bombings of the harbour. So the hospital was rapidly moved to an open space inland where the red cross could be displayed far away from anything anyone might wish to bomb.

The nurses who were to staff the hospital had not yet arrived from England. As yet only two lots of nurses had landed and both were for hospitals in Algiers. Here male orderlies still carried on. You couldn't get a wash because no one had any soap or towels to spare. Ten days without a wash is unpleasant. Though the doctors (who on the voyage out had lectured so severely about the importance of hygiene in countries like this) seemed amazingly unconcerned about it now. People wash too much, anyway, one of them said when someone mentioned this. There was one urinal bottle between two tents, and the same number of orderlies. This involved some intricate timing to get the bottle within twenty minutes of needing it, and to get rid of it afterwards. You couldn't put it down, there was no room between the beds. Anyway, it would not stand up, it wasn't designed to do so. On one occasion a man had to hold it in one hand while he ate lunch with the other. Thirty-five minutes it was before he got rid of it, they timed him. Like a nightmare relay race in which no one will receive the baton.

In the bed on his right there was a French officer who spent the time teaching himself English. He became a nuisance because he would keep leaning across to ask how words were pronounced.

'Muzzer?'

'Mother.'

'Murther.'

'No. *Mother*.'

'Muvver.'

'No. MOTHER. MOTHER.'

'Murzzer.'

So it would go on. He was a nice fellow, and setting everyone a fine example, but his ineffective diligence was maddening. He said he was an artist, and you said he was lucky: in a situation like this he could work. Someone should be able to get hold of some paper and crayons, if not brush and paint. He said it wasn't a question of paint and brushes, but that there was nothing to paint.

You look down the long brown tent; at the hurt filthy figures lying on the baby-blue beds packed closely together; and at the far end where a brilliant beam of sunlight blazed through the end of the tent, brilliantly lighting the end two beds.

'If I were a painter I would paint that.'

'But I am a romantic painter,' he said.

'I thought you people were supposed to be the logical, we the romantic race.'

All day long they kept taking away men to the operating theatre, and when they came back they behaved as though they were drunk: it was the effect of the anaesthetic. Whenever they came for another body the eyes of the others would roll round like the eyes of animals in a slaughter-house. It was a mixed ward with officers and other ranks, the sick and the wounded all jumbled up. A few beds away there was a Cockney private who hardly stopped talking for two days. It was impossible to catch what he said because he was some way away, but from the whining grumbling tone of voice he seemed to have a grievance that took a lot of airing. He ended every sentence with a pause followed by the words 'bloo'y bahstard,' and each time you hoped this was the end of the incoherent grumble. But it never was, and you began to think he must have been badly wounded and had a hard-luck story. When they took him away – on the second day, luckily – it transpired that he was a driver attached to a unit not very far from the hospital. All that was wrong with him was that his face had come out in a rash. So far as you could make out there was no one with measles.

Those who were less severely wounded were left alone. The doctors said the new thing was to change dressings as little as possible, the longer they were left the quicker the wounds healed.

The third day it was possible to wash your face, a minute bowl of water was produced, but no shaving kit was available and for the first time you had a beard. The French officer continued to study English relentlessly, and the only relief from helping him with his pronunciation was when they came to do his wound – his was one they did occasionally look at. He had a deep cut in the thigh which looked like a lascivious, heavily made-up harlot mouth with the lips parted. It was almost a Toulouse-Lautrec mouth, that wound.

One afternoon a young airman came in. He had been burned on the arms. His wrists and forearms were tightly bandaged and he held them before him, dangling. Like the fore-paws of a kangaroo. He looked nineteen. He had straw-coloured hair, long thin bird-nose, hard blue eyes that seemed to have been forced far back in the sockets. He had come in to see one of the doctors. From their conversation it appeared that he was being flown back to England. After they had finished talking he walked slowly through to the far end of the tent, staring strangely and fixedly to his front. Walking thus, so slim in his blue uniform, with helpless hands bound and dangling in front of his chest, he looked like a demented angel. The eyes of the wounded rolled round, following his strained, painful walk, wishing, no doubt, that they were going to be flown back to England too.

When the aching wound and the bombers had marked the fourth sundown, an orderly came in and announced that a number of walking wounded, including you, would be leaving for Algiers in the morning.

Stations are always exciting but Bône was especially so. A turmoil of troops, civilians, and wounded. Arab boys clamouring to buy and sell. Steam and whistles: goods trains loaded with guns, elderly black engines driven by English and American soldiers. And the hospital train, ghostly white and decorated with the Red Cross. Movement and shouting and bustle: and the wounded who couldn't walk patiently waiting on their stretchers. It was like a scene from *Cavalcade*, with Arab trimmings.

A group of elderly women, dressed in black, were in tears and softly moaning: 'Ah, *les pauvres blessés! Les pauvres blessés!*'

To be a *pauvre blessé* is wonderful. The only time all the world loves you. One of the old women raised a wrinkled hand and threw a flower. She hadn't the strength to throw it more than a yard or two, so you limped over and picked it up with some difficulty – it was still hard for you to bend – and she began to cry quite hard, while the others continued to moan softly. One of them kissed her finger-tips and touched your sleeve with them: you thanked them and smiled your way out of it before you started crying yourself. Perhaps they were thinking of names like Ypres and Somme, those old women in black.

As you stood there, bearded and dirty – one trouser leg missing to make room for the bandage which encased you thickly from thigh to calf – a Guards sergeant approached. These Guardsmen were on their way to the front for the first time and they were still meticulously clean and smart. The sergeant's great arm swept into a salute with the smooth gigantic delicacy of a locomotive piston. He presented his sympathy and good wishes. It was rough up there from what he had heard. He bet it was. Your lot had done a fine job, from what he had heard. A very fine job indeed. It hadn't been at all pleasant, from what he had heard. He hoped the wound would soon clear up. He then produced from his breast pocket a squashed packet containing three Woodbines.

'These'll be more use to you than to me, sir,' he said.

You said no, he must keep them. But he wouldn't hear of it. You thanked him. He stiffened. Threw another overwhelming salute, wished you luck, and right-about-turned himself away to where his unit were grouped. You couldn't beat being a *pauvre blessé*.

After a while the busy little Movement Control officers started shepherding the wounded aboard the hospital train, and incongruously a sapper corporal climbed into the cab of the engine to drive it. You had a last look round the absorbing scene that was so like something out of *Cavalcade*, and then you made your way to the coach reserved for walking wounded officers. There was more shouting: then, with a great hissing of steam, the elderly engine

46

jerked into motion. As the train rolled slowly out of the station the moaning of the old women swelled into crescendo of 'Les pauvres blessés' and 'Bon voyage' – as though the platform barrier was their wailing wall. You wondered if they spent their days permanently at the station, thinking, perhaps, of names like Ypres and Somme.

The train consisted of an odd assortment of coaches, some of which had been converted to take stretcher cases. The coach for walking wounded officers was comfortable and had the charm inseparable from faded gentility. The woodwork was shabby but rich in the remains of fancy inlay: the pale grey upholstery was worn and grubby but bore unmistakable traces of former splendour. This, you felt, was the sort of coach in which a Hapsburg might have travelled half a century before.

No one seemed to know when the train would reach Algiers. Least of all the little doctor in charge of it. 'Sometime tomorrow afternoon,' he said airily. From the beginning the train made frequent stops, apparently for no reason, and between stops it moved slowly. It soon became clear that time schedules meant nothing to it. It wasn't that kind of train. It would amble along like this perhaps for days, and some time or other it would arrive. It was always the same with these hospital trains, an old hand said.

The M.O. in charge was a chubby, grey-haired captain wearing First-War ribbons. He loved his train: the best, he told you, of all these North African hospital trains. He proved to be one of those mild little men who breathe fire. He constantly referred to 'the last lot', by which he meant the other war. 'In the last lot we shot deserters, and no nonsense.' The shooting of deserters appeared to be a particular obsession with him, and he lost little time in bringing the subject up. But almost equally soon it became evident that if you were prepared to listen to his view the reward was a liberal share of the whisky with which his private compartment (he called it his surgery) was well supplied. Once you had adjusted yourself to the tempo of this train, and had made friends with the little doctor, the time began to pass pleasantly enough. At least this was better than the brown hospital tent. It was not till the train had been meandering for nearly an hour that the Doc had let out the news that there was a German officer on it. Sheldon had noticed a compartment marked reserved and with the blinds drawn. He had assumed that it was for a *blessé* who was either very eminent or highly infectious and he had forgotten about it. That, it turned out, was for the German. 'In case,' the doctor explained, 'you fellows objected to travelling with a Hun. In the last lot there used to be strong feelings about that sort of thing'. You had laughed and said how silly: the little doctor seemed surprised.

For the first time since the war began you had a chance to meet the enemy as a person. It was the most memorable feature of the strange journey on the meandering hospital train.

How strangely impersonal to the soldier is that figure – essential to any war – the Enemy. To begin with he is an abstract idea: an idea in textbooks and lectures existing solely as an accessory to a puzzle. When you study the technique of attack, the Enemy is the shrewd defensive layout which exposes the weakness of your play. When you're working on defence, he is the mocking laughter of your teacher, the theory which rips your defensive efforts to shreds.

Baring your teeth – like the mild little train doctor and the Battle School hearties – and calling the enemy 'The Hun' didn't really help. It didn't make the Enemy personal: it merely made the abstract idea rather ridiculous.

The position admittedly changed when you started fighting. There was nothing abstract about an enemy who was shooting at you. He became real enough then. But still he wasn't *people*. He was still impersonal: a powerful collective, a form of danger whose guns seemed to shoot faster, whose shells seemed to burst with an uglier sound. The name 'Boche' seemed to suggest this in an odd way – it was the only one of the vernacular nicknames Sheldon found it easy to take to. But calling this hidden poker, this invisible collective, 'Jerry' – as the soldiers continued to do – turned it into no more than a charming fiction: a cartoon character.

'Good morning – or rather good afternoon,' the German said

when Sheldon entered the compartment.

'Hello. My name's Sheldon.'

'Meissendorfer. Luftwaffe.'

He was wounded in the jaw and also in the right leg. He lay along one side of the compartment, a little awkwardly, with the bad leg on the seat, the other on the floor.

'You don't look too comfortable. Can I give you a hand?'

'I thank you, no. This is the only position I can manage. My head. I cannot bend it very well.'

'You speak English well. I'm afraid I don't know a word of your language,' Sheldon said, and was immediately amused at the pat way the Englishman's language apology had slipped out.

'I was two years at Bristol University studying architecture. You know Bristol?'

'No.'

Sheldon estimated that the German was three or four years older than himself, probably about twenty-eight.

'Where were you shot down?'

'Near Oued Zrir. I ran into some Spitfires. They're good, those Spitfires.' They might have been couple of motorists, Sheldon thought, the Mercedes man paying his respects to a Bentley owner.

They continued to talk with a rather careful politeness. Chiefly about England. Like many Germans Meissendorfer was an indefatigable tourist. He had not wasted his years in England. He spoke affectionately of the Lake District – which Sheldon had never visited – and that led to Wordsworth whom he admired, so he said, more than any other English poet. His special interest in architecture had led him, it seemed, to at least half of the cathedral cities. Then they had got on to music.

Sheldon was finding the experience stimulating. To begin with there was the rather enjoyable melodrama of the situation: officers who were enemies, both wounded in action, closeted together in a formal discussion of the fugues of Bach and the comparative merits of Winchester and Salisbury cathedrals. But also, Sheldon was realising, this was the first grown-up conversation he had had with anybody for longer than he could remember.

'You married?' Sheldon asked at one point.

'No. It is better not to be married in war.'

'Sometimes I think that, sometimes I don't. It must be nice to know there's someone who cares whether you come back or not. But it has its disadvantages.'

'This is my girl,' the German said, fumbling in his pocket. Before he had found the snapshot Sheldon knew that she would be blonde, healthy-looking, and in white shorts. She was – and very pretty.

'She is a fine glider pilot,' Meissendorfer said fondly.

'But can she cook?'

'All German girls can cook.'

So the conversation had proceeded. Only once did politics come up.

'We shouldn't be at war, England and Germany,' Meissendorfer had said.

'You can hardly say that it is our fault that we are,' Sheldon replied.

'You needn't have come in.'

'What about Poland?'

'That is different. If we had not gone to war they would have attacked us with the Russians.'

'So you believe all that.'

'It is true. You do not know these Poles and Russians as we do.'

'Propaganda!' Sheldon said.

'No,' Meissendorfer had said, 'this is not propaganda, I have seen things on the Russian front – seen things with my own eyes that you would not believe. You do not know the Russians. They are not like you and us.' It was said without emotion; a simple statement of fact. It would be abortive, Sheldon thought, to pursue the matter now. The German, it seemed, felt the same. Neither of them spoke for some time. It was Meissendorfer who broke the silence.

'I like your system of government,' he said with the air of a connoisseur who has gone deeply into the matter and has not lightly arrived at his conclusion. 'But of course, it would not do for us,' he added as an afterthought.

'Why not?'

'We Germans respect authority. If we had your kind of democracy there would not be three or four but at least a hundred political parties. Every man would start his own.'

'All the same you might give it a try some time.'

That was as near as they came to the discussion of the deeper issues that had led to their meeting. It was some time later that Meissendorfer asked about London.

'How is London? It was always my favourite European capital.'

'Still pretty good. What you people have left of it.'

'Dear old London,' Meissendorfer said wistfully. 'Cap Gris-Nez – Sevenoaks – Turn left for Victoria.'

'You were in the Blitz then?'

'Yes. But I knew it well before the war.'

'My home is in London.'

'I hope it is not damaged.' He seemed perfectly sincere.

'Not yet. But not for want of trying.'

'Please?'

'It has had some narrow escapes.'

'Your family lives there?'

'I have no family, my parents are both dead. It is a flat. I let it for the duration.'

It didn't occur to Sheldon at the time that this was a strange subject to be discussing, without feeling, in this way. It was simply talking shop. That they were on opposite sides seemed incidental to the circumstances that they were both soldiers, both in the same line of business, young men who, having known the same strains, frustrations and dangers, had met through the common experience of being wounded. Only the uniforms happened to be different. Between them they shared a secret unspoken knowledge. So that they seemed almost to have more in common with each other than either had with those of his own kind who were not soldiers, and perhaps that is one of the subtlest evils of war.

This instinctive easy communion between them was pinpointed by a remark the German passed when they were in one of the bouts of shop-talk. He was describing the circumstances which preceded the departure of his squadron for North Africa.

'First we were supposed to be going to the Eastern Front and we were given special winter clothing. Then they sent us to Foggia in southern Italy, where they took away the winter clothes and gave us tropical kit. They said it was to Rommel in Libya. Then it was changed again and we were sent here at short notice – there was no time to change the kit before we left. So we arrived in the coldest part of the winter with tropical stuff, and it was two days before it was changed.

'It was a typical German Army ball-up,' Meissendorfer added.

For Sheldon that comment – with its reassuring reminder that the infallible German military machine was in the end no different from any other – completed the metamorphosis of the Enemy from an abstraction into a person: a person not at all unlike himself.

After leaving the German's compartment Sheldon had walked slowly past the doctor's compartment hoping to be invited in for a drink. The hint wasn't necessary. The doctor, now pleasantly sozzled, was awaiting him impatiently, agog with curiosity.

'What happened? What was it like? What did he say?'

'He didn't bite,' Sheldon said.

FIVE

AT ALGIERS a new phase of being wounded began. Algiers was Head Office, Capital City, Leavetown. Glamorous, sordid, beautiful, noisy, vast, crowded, glittering, desirable Leavetown. The antithetical quintessence of town which the soldier craves in his exile to bare hillside and hole in the ground.

But the first taste was tormentingly brief. A glimpse through the window as the hospital bus busily groaned its way in low gear up the rue Michelet, the handsome main street which climbs through half a dozen hairpin turns from the heart of the port to the beautiful residential areas up on the hill. There was a kaleidoscope impression of dense military traffic ceaselessly choking the crowded streets; of three-car trams, teeming within, festooned without, with Arabs, so that you wondered how anyone inside the cars escaped or collected a fare; of mysterious smells in which garlic and charcoal and betel could be identified; of ships, warehouses, shops, offices, alleys, steps, cafes, cinemas, and tier upon tier of pretty red-roofed white houses rising steeply to the peak of the hill which towered above the harbour. Then a gateway swallowed up the bus; Leavetown became a forbidden wonder; you were in the white hospital.

This hospital was quite different from the other. It was large and light and antiseptic; a real hospital. The ward, which contained twelve well-separated beds, was airy and cheerlessly white. There was a washroom and lavatory close by. Not American plumbing, of course. The lavatory was strictly hole-in-the-floor, but deluxe hole-in-the-floor: tiles, porcelain, and footrests. And there were nurses, female nurses from England. It was so different from the long brown tent, and almost from the first moment in this great white hospital you realised that something had ended. You were no longer a *pauvre blessé*. Just a *blessé*. There was a big difference.

You had become a case in a well-run institution that had little to do with the war. The man on your left had fallen off a motorcycle in Algiers, the one on your right was getting over influenza. You were just another temperature to take, pulse to feel, dressing to examine and sometimes change. Just another case to be awakened at the earliest moment of an interminable day so that your comfortable bed could be rendered tidily uncomfortable. In the days since leaving the front you had exhausted your capacity for sleep: you were sated with it now, like a man who has gorged himself too well at a longed-for feast. The clean, white bed, which ten days before had seemed the ultimate bliss, was already a cell in an antiseptic prison. With all day and all night in which to sleep, and a comfortable bed in which to do so, the last thing you wanted any more was sleep. You could walk well enough now to hobble to the lavatory, you fretted to be allowed to go on out into the town and have some fun. But they wouldn't hear of it, and any possibility of going out unofficially was effectively prevented by the fact that your only trousers were the ones in which you had arrived, the ones with a leg missing. So you fretted through those first few days in which the boredom seemed to be relieved only by the regularly repeated daily annoyances: the preposterously early awakening and making of the bed: the indifferent meals: the constant taking of the temperature: the visit of the padre. Of these by far the most trying was the padre.

He was a small, black-haired, bird of a man who always came in as though he were already late for six other more important appointments and was fitting you in at great inconvenience.

'Couldn't go out without popping my head round the door – though my goodness! I must get a move on. How are you all this morning? As if I can't see for myself! Getting better every day, I can see that, yes, I can see that all right! My, how you've all improved! Well, if there's anything I can do, remember you've only got to ask. Cheerio, fellows, cheerio!' and he'd be through the door before anyone had a chance to ask for anything. So one morning, timing it carefully, Sheldon had said, 'Yes, there was something – I would like something to read. I would be much obliged if you could produce some books.' Caught on one foot – literally – the padre said, 'Yes, of course.' Then recovered himself and swiftly added that he couldn't definitely promise anything, books were frightfully scarce, everyone wanted them – but he would try.

The next morning Sheldon asked him how he had got on.

'Books. Ah, yes, my dear fellow, of course. Silly of me. I had it with me.' He left the ward and was back a few moments later with a paper-backed thriller which he handed to Sheldon.

'*There* we are, my dear fellow!' Sheldon saw at once that the last thirty pages or so had been torn out, one at a time. He was about to hand it back to the padre with the suggestion that the book would now be more useful in the place from which the padre had removed it, but the little man was too quick for him – he was through the door before Sheldon had even opened his mouth to speak.

There was the usual banter with the nurses to help pass the time. Most of it was directed at Sister O'Donnell, one of those red-haired sportive Irish nurses of which there seems always to be one on every hospital staff. The other sisters came in for their share, too; all, that is, except Sister Murgatroyd. Sister Murgatroyd was the best-looking of them, but there was something slightly severe in her manner which restrained even the boldest of the ward teasers from taking liberties with her. They had decided that she was cold and they left her alone.

Sheldon took little part in this badinage, mainly because he disliked the other five officers in the half-empty ward. He could find nothing in common with any of them, and in his bored, fretful state of mind he made little effort to disguise this. Any resentment they might have felt towards him was kept under control, however, as he happened to be the only battle-casualty among them. This gave him a privileged seclusion of which he was glad to take advantage. They seemed content to leave him alone – probably writing him off as a moody cuss who was battle 'happy' – while they vied with one another to provoke the spirited Celtic repartee of Sister O'Donnell. Left thus to himself, Sheldon found himself becoming aware of Sister Murgatroyd.

She was certainly not beautiful: there was a hint of coarseness about her skin that precluded that. Nor was she pretty – she had too much character. But she was undeniably good-looking: with wide grey eyes, a broadish nose slightly upturning, and a full firm mouth. She spoke little, and always to the point, in a low musical voice, and this enhanced the sense of character and even power which her presence radiated. Her looks were the kind that grow on a man because there is something behind them, something not immediately apparent. So the days, long and empty, passed slowly in the white antiseptic vacuum, and there were only the appearances of Sister Murgatroyd to which to look forward.

For motionless stretches of time Sheldon would lie on his back thinking dreamily about nothing. He was surprised to find how easy it was to think of absolutely nothing. He made an effort to write, but a few short letters to brother officers and friends at home were all he could manage: though he was normally a man who poured himself into long letters to chosen friends – the sort of letters that are written seldom but at great length and are kept and re-read by their recipients. He again attempted to start a diary: throughout the war he had been doing that, telling himself that it was silly not to keep some kind of daily journal, that a war diary, however sketchy, would make fascinating reading in years to come. Yet once again, with all the time in the world at his disposal, he could not concentrate sufficiently, could not interest himself enough in what he was recording to keep on with it.

It was the same with reading. He had found – not long after the book episode with the padre – that one of the surgeons in another division of the hospital had brought a great number of books with him and was willing to lend them. Here was the supreme opportunity to read some of those classics one had somehow never got round to. Gibbon would have been ideal, this was just the time to tackle Gibbon! The *Decline and Fall*, however, was not available and he decided to study *Hamlet* – he might even learn the damn thing by heart. He already knew it fairly well, but to come out of hospital knowing it by heart really would be something. But he found it hard to read. Before he had completed even a single reading he had had to put it down, turning instead to a volume of Chesterton's essays.

These terse, brittle, argumentative, witty little pieces might jerk his mind into life! But again he could not get stuck into them. He tried reading the book straight through and then he dipped at random, but it was no good. So he turned to poetry: perhaps that would be more in tune with the emotional mood of his present situation.

The books the doctor had sent up included a Palgrave. But the volume had to open by chance at Lovelace's 'To Lucasta, On Going to the Wars', and at once be became depressed and filled with self-pity because he had no Lucasta: not even the nunnery of Julie's chaste breast, the little bitch, he thought savagely. It was no good, everyone had to have a Lucasta, you couldn't get away from it. So he closed the Palgrave and turned in desperation to a couple of early Evelyn Waughs, but neither of them seemed nearly as funny as he remembered them to have been when he first read them before the war. He gave up for the time being the idea of reading. It troubled him that even the capacity for that pleasure seemed to have gone.

Was it the same with other people? Did soldiering do this to you? Was it the systematic reduction of living to an animal business of existence and survival? Or was it because of not having a Lucasta? The null uselessness of the wireless transmitter that lacks a receiving station with which to connect? The aloneness of the automatous man who has mastered a repugnant technique of existence but is denied the compensating impetus of love that alone can make it seem worthwhile? It must be that. Lucasta. There had to be someone for whom you were doing it.

He was becoming increasingly aware of Sister Murgatroyd, and during her brief purposeful visits to the ward his eyes scarcely left her. There is a limited number of motions through which a nurse can go in the course of routine ward duties, and he knew Sister Murgatroyd's by heart, and in her absence his mind lingered on them all by turns. The swift entrance and the instinctive manner of closing the door noiselessly; the wrist flick, firm but graceful, with which she shook the thermometer back to zero, and the lift of her head when she held the instrument up to read it; her faintly reproving way of patting the creases in the bed-clothes, and the scarcely perceptible panting as she jerked at the sheets and blankets; the easy balance with which she managed two or more trays at meal times; the way she would pause, lips slightly parted, one hand on her hip, and sweep the ward with a final stock-taking glance before leaving; and, when she was satisfied that nothing had been overlooked, the regal swish of her skirt with which she would move to the door, not hurrying, yet seeming to arrive there quickly.

Watching her perform these same simple movements and actions several times a day, he realised that what distinguished her above all from the others was her sense of *style*. She invested the simplest of her professional actions with it. She brought a proud, graceful efficiency to everything she did. She had the grace of the superb craftsman, so that her performance of the dullest, most menial of chores became a deliberate and attractive expression of herself. She was completely the mistress of her trade, the trade of nursing, and through her skill she achieved a serenity and beauty which elevated craft almost to the level of art: even the manipulation of a thermometer or a dirty bandage became an act of style and beauty.

So it seemed to the jaded, bored Sheldon as he lay for hour after hour staring at the white ceiling. When he was well enough to get up for an hour or two – instead of merely to visit the lavatory – he took to wandering about the corridors and the other wards and to hanging about the Sisters' office in the hope of running into her. But it was typical of her that you never seemed to catch her, as you did the others, gossiping in one of the passages, or resting for a minute or two with a newspaper in the Sisters' office. If you met her at all – and it was maddening how much time she appeared to spend in other parts of the hospital – she always seemed to be hurrying from somewhere to somewhere else. After she had evaded him for two hours one afternoon he thought, quite suddenly: 'Damn you, Sister Murgatroyd, I think I've fallen for you.' That evening, when she leaned across him to smooth the bed-clothes, he had the greatest difficulty in resisting an impulse to pull her fiercely down and scald her with kisses. At that moment the padre came in, and in an excess of frustration and bad temper Sheldon called the chaplain over.

'Look, Padre, you're always asking what you can do for us. If you want to make yourself really useful will you try and get hold of some whisky. I don't care what it costs.'

The birdface cocked an eyebrow. The lips pursed in roguish reproof.

'Alas, my dear fellow, your request hardly falls within my province as – er – guardian of the spiritual welfare of the hospital. Though in a manner of speaking I – er – suppose what you ask for is – ha-ha – in a sense spiritual welfare! Alas! I cannot help you there.'

'Oh, go and stuff your spiritual welfare!' Sheldon snapped. 'Sorry, Sister,' he added. He noticed that though the mouth was composed, as always, a little severely, the grey eyes were smiling.

When she came in later the same evening with his supper there was a small medicine bottle on the tray.

'It's a tonic,' she said. 'You're to take it after the evening meal now that you're getting better.'

When he had finished his supper he uncorked the bottle and found that it was filled with whisky. When she came in to collect the supper trays he made as if to thank her, but she stopped him with one of those barely perceptible but eloquent tremors of the lips in which she specialised. So he scribbled a note instead and left it on his tray.

'Dear Sister Murgatroyd,' he wrote, 'you are the dearest person in all the world. Beg borrow or steal me a pair of trousers (with two legs) and I will take you out and buy you the finest dinner in all Algiers'.

Next morning the face of Sister Murgatroyd – calm and impassive as usual – trembled momentarily towards a smile, and as he sat with his mouth full of thermometer he felt very happy: when, shortly afterwards, he returned from his morning visit to the washroom to discover a brand-new pair of trousers over the back of his chair, he felt even happier. And when the doctor, on his morning rounds, said he could now start going out if he wanted, he was as close as he would probably ever be to hysteria.

With the arrival of the trousers and permission to make use of them, the final phase of Being Wounded had begun. It was two weeks since his arrival: it had seemed more like two months.

As soon as he had dressed he hurried across to the Sisters' mess hoping to catch her alone, but the place was stiff with nurses and she had to come outside to talk, and even then people were constantly passing. The lack of privacy is in the end the worst thing of all, he thought.

'I'm a free man. Dinner tonight,' he said.

'Sorry, not tonight.'

'Please.'

'I'm on duty.'

'Get out of it.'

'I can't.'

'There must be a way. Say it's your grandmother's funeral, or something.'

'I haven't got a grandmother.'

'Change with somebody else.'

'I can't.'

'Oh, hell. I was so looking forward.'

'I'm sorry.'

'I don't want to go out now.'

'You'll have more fun on your own, the first time.'

'Can't you possibly do a swap with someone?'

'I'm afraid not.'

'Oh, hell.'

'I'm very sorry. I'd have loved to. Another time, perhaps. I must go now.'

'Tomorrow, then?'

'Perhaps. I'll try and work it.'

'When will you know?'

'In the morning. I really must go. There are casualties in this hospital.'

'Tomorrow, then. Without fail. Please.'

'I'll try and know definitely when I come and tuck you in tonight. Take it easy today. It's your first time out, remember. Don't overdo it. G'bye.' She was away before he could say another word.

He found a truck that was going into the town and joined an assorted collection of soldiers in the back of it. It was exciting, the first liberation: like the end of term at school. Perhaps after all the dinner date would keep till tomorrow. It might be as well to have made a recce first. From the truck he went straight to the Field Cashier. It was fun to be in possession of money again: for weeks he hadn't even seen any. Where he had been it was merely paper.

The town thrilled him with its noise, smells, colour, and congestion. For a time he just wandered, pausing frequently to stand and watch. No wonder simple men delight in standing on street corners. The stream of life is the most permanently available of free entertainments. No wonder it is the main pleasure of poor men. The soldier is a poor man, too – in a way. So he adores street corners and the towns of which they are the focal points. The soldier's pleasures are simple and direct. They are merely the antithesis of his discomforts, which are also simple and direct.

After cold water he wants hot; after barren ground, the crowded town; after the mess-tin, clean china; after the sentry's loneliness, crowds; after filth, cleanliness (the combat soldier never has to be ordered to smarten up as does his home-service brother – he does it automatically); after mud he wants pavements; after a world consisting of men he wants a woman.

The town – any town – is the answer, and the success of the town is purely a matter of degree. It just has to be a town – Nuneaton or Winchester or Algiers or Alexandria. They are all the answer at different times to different soldiers. And whether the soldier is young or old, sensitive or coarse, intelligent or simple, after a period of combat his parched consciousness craves town – town, not *the* town – as desperately as a parched body thirsts for water.

On this first day Sheldon wandered and loitered and gazed. He left the main roads and explored the side streets, the courtyards, the squares, the steps, and some of the passages and alleys; though to his disappointment whenever he came on one that was particularly enticing it was invariably marked 'Out Of Bounds'. He more than once regretted the uniform which placed beyond his reach the mysterious inner heart of the town. The craving for total contrast is a conditioning of the soldier's mind that he cannot dispel: after the antiseptic whiteness of the incarcerating hospital, the exotic squalor of the dark, out-of-bounds native sections was difficult to resist, and when in due course he came to the Officers' Club, its relentless conformity with every other Officers' Club he had ever been in filled him at first with a deep feeling of bathos.

In the bar he got talking with a major in the Ordnance Corps. After they had had several drinks this man, whose name was Crawshaw, said why not go back with him and have dinner in the mess. They went off in Crawshaw's Utility, and the mess turned out to be in a large house halfway up the hill. The entrance to the house was rich in orange trees and bougainvillaea, and inside it was sumptuously pseudo-Moorish.

'You do yourselves well,' Sheldon said.

'It's not too bad.'

A large red-faced colonel walked over and Crawshaw introduced Sheldon to him.

'Slumming, eh?' the colonel said. 'Come to see how the poor live?'

'The poor seem to be doing fine,' Sheldon said.

'Rather,' the colonel said. 'I suppose it all seems a bit much to chaps like you.'

'I'm all for making oneself as comfortable as possible,' Sheldon said.

'Exactly, old boy,' the colonel said. He seemed relieved. 'I mean to say it wouldn't do you chaps if we slept on nails. Now, would it?'

The colonel excused himself.

The dinner was excellent. Army ration stew – in apparently unlimited quantity – skilfully converted into a goulash. Sheldon wasn't surprised to learn that the mess secretary was a Catering Corps captain who was at the Savoy until he was called up.

They were a curious lot, these H.Q. people: they had the glossy, confident look of successful business men, Sheldon thought. Rotarians in uniform, that's what they were. Much of the talk concerned rackets. Everyone, it seemed had a private racket of some sort, and there seemed to be a good deal of hearty competition as to whose was going best. A lot of it was incomprehensible to Sheldon. But during the evening he did learn that Crawshaw's special interest was lipstick.

'There's an awful lot of good lipstick in this country,' Crawshaw said seriously. 'The real stuff: French and Italian. I've spent a lot of time going round the neighbouring towns and villages buying up every bit I can. I've got well over a couple of thousand now. When I get 'em back home they'll be worth money.'

'But will you be able to get them back?'

'Oh, yes,' Crawshaw said. 'There are always ways and means.'

'It's a funny war,' Sheldon said.

When the white-coated civilian waiters had served coffee Sheldon all of a sudden couldn't stand it any longer. He sought out Crawshaw and pretended that his leg was hurting him. Crawshaw at once offered to run him back to the hospital.

So that was how 'they' lived. It's funny, Sheldon thought as he walked up the hospital stairs. That fellow gets a shilling a day more than me because he's on the staff. It's really very funny.

As he passed the Sisters' office he saw through the open door that Sister Murgatroyd was inside checking laundry.

'Oh, it's you,' she said.

'Hello.'

'You're very late,' she said severely. 'You weren't meant to stay out so long your first time.'

'I had to drown my sorrows.'

'Which sorrows are those?' she asked, mocking.

'You know damn well which sorrows.'

'It's very silly to overdo it the first time. You might easily set your leg off again.'

'Stop being a nurse and be a woman for a change.'

'It's against regulations.'

'If I say I've missed you all day I suppose you'll say that's against regulations too.'

'Borderline case. I'm very flattered. By the way, tomorrow's off.'

'Oh, no.'

'I'm afraid so. It's infuriating. But there's been a rush of new arrivals. A train-load came in this afternoon. None of us will be able to get out for at least two days.'

'Wasn't there any warning?'

'No. It's always like that. We never know how many are coming. One minute we're half empty, the next we've twice as many as we can cope with.'

'This would happen to me.'

'It isn't much fun for us either: sixteen-hour stretches of duty, very little sleep, no time off to relax.' She said it quietly.

'I'm sorry,' he said. 'I didn't mean that. I was just terribly disappointed. It'll be hellish for you during the next two days. If I know you, it will be more like twenty-four hours at a stretch.'

'It's our job,' she said. 'You must go to bed. You should have been in bed hours ago.'

'Yes, nurse.' He walked up to her and kissed her very gently on the lips. 'Goodnight, Lucasta.'

'Why Lucasta?'

'I thought you said your name was Lucasta.'

'You're drunk,' she said.

Sheldon had been too tired to brood on his disappointment that night. He was instantly asleep and slept deeply. By morning he was resigned to the fact that he must exclude Sister Murgatroyd from his plans for two days, and determined to find alternative distraction. By lunchtime he was in the bar at the Officers' Club – the turmoil caused by the new batch of hospital arrivals making it easy for the old hands, like himself, to slip out early without anyone caring or even noticing. After three pink gins he found himself in conversation with a Captain Slythe, of the R.A.S.C.

Slythe was a seedy-looking man with a blotchy face, a straggling parody of a military moustache, and a greasy peaked cap pulled exaggeratedly down at the sides in the cause, no doubt, of a racy appearance. He had quickly picked Sheldon out as a tourist.

'Care to see the sights? I live here,' he said. He wasn't, perhaps, the companion of one's choice, but he seemed friendly enough, and he had transport. Everything, Sheldon was rapidly discovering, depended on having transport in this place. With it a subaltern was a millionaire, without it a general was less than nothing. And no one was more sensitive to its value than the available ladies.

They lunched together and afterwards, as it was a fine day, and the pink gins had induced a desire for fresh air, Slythe drove him for an hour or so round and about the town. Then they returned to the Officers' Club and dozed until six, when the bar opened again. After they had had three or four drinks Captain Slythe suggested a visit to Chez Suzy, an establishment to which Sheldon had heard a number of officers refer with a smirk.

'After what you've been through, you must be in need of female company.'

Sheldon thought it might be amusing. No one else cared whether he had a good time or not, so he agreed that it was an excellent idea. After a short drive, Captain Slythe parked the Utility in a unit car park which was guarded; removed the distributor from the ignition coil; and led the way through an alley, up some steps, along a side street, and into a building that resembled a third-rate commercial hotel fallen on hard times.

'It's not exactly Paris, old man, but the girls aren't bad. And they're clean.'

In the vestibule an old hawk-faced woman, dressed in the traditional black, sat behind a desk. As they entered she rose and came to meet them.

'*Officiers, ce soir,*' she squeaked at them, peering accusingly at their insignia of rank.

'*Oui, oui. Compris,*' said Captain Slythe brushing past her towards the desk. 'The system, old man, is that they dole it out in units of a quarter of an hour.'

'I leave it to you. You know the form.'

'Frankly, I usually make do with half an hour. It isn't Paris. I've known romantic types, though, who wouldn't look at less than a couple of hours.'

'Let's make it half an hour,' Sheldon said. It was hard to think of the project as anything but a joke. The atmosphere of the place was enough to dispel any erotic longing the moment you stepped inside.

The old woman had hobbled back behind the desk, and Slythe gave her two thousand francs. In return she gave him four large tiddly-winks, two of which he handed to Sheldon.

'Receipts, old man. Each one worth a quarter of an hour. You give 'em to the girl as you go in. On her way home she exchanges them for cash here. Good system. Saves a lot of book keeping.'

They went up the creaking staircase – which was covered with dark-green linoleum – and Slythe led the way to a waiting-room. They might have been at a downtown dentist's. Shabby chairs, table littered with dog-eared newspapers and magazines. There were three officers already waiting: a bald middle-aged English captain, a plump American major, and a studious-looking English subaltern. They were studiedly pretending to be unaware of one another, and only the subaltern furtively stole a glance at the new arrivals as they entered the room.

'Ask for Hilda,' Captain Slythe had advised on the way up. After they had been there five minutes or so the door opened and an enormous brown woman strolled in and glared at each of them in turn. She was naked except for a thin cotton robe which hung open at the front; a cigarette dangled from one corner of her mouth. Sheldon was relieved that she wasn't Hilda. Without any word being spoken the bald English captain put down his magazine and followed the brown woman out. Shortly after this there was an incomprehensible screech from upstairs. The American tossed his paper onto the table and went off in pursuit of the screech.

'I'll give Hilda a shout,' Captain Slythe said and disappeared. While he was gone a coarse, stubby little Negro girl put her head round the door, and the subaltern's face lit up. Sheldon began to fear the worst. Captain Slythe reappeared.

'Hilda's ready when you are, old man. She was having a smoke. It's the end room on the right. Mine's upstairs. See you later. *Vive l'amour!*'

The door was open and Hilda, a short, stocky Frenchwoman with a snub nose and a black fringe beckoned Sheldon in as if she were impatient to get the whole thing over as quickly as possible. She neither smiled nor spoke; she merely nodded when he handed her the tiddly-winks, which she placed in a jar on the mantelpiece. As he undressed he noticed that there was a wash-basin and a broad, hard-looking divan covered with a sheet, but without bed-clothes. Sex seemed strangely remote. He became suddenly aware of all the perils, so diligently impressed on the army, and was glad he had remembered to provide himself with the equipment he now removed from his fob pocket. So it was a complete surprise when, as soon as he had undressed, Hilda seized him firmly, marched him over to the wash-basin, which she had filled with warm water, and washed him thoroughly. Whatever thoughts he might have had on the subject, Hilda wasn't taking any chances either. This hygienic preliminary over, she went straight over to the bed, and lay on her back staring, without expression, at the ceiling.

Sheldon was by this time so disinterested – and so, apparently, was she – that he longed to say: 'Look, let us just smoke a cigarette together and then I'll go.' But he knew this was out of the question. Even at this level there must be professional pride. He couldn't back out at this stage. He removed his glasses and steeled himself. Yet the longer he lay with her the less likely did it seem that the occasion could achieve fulfilment, and her efforts to correct this were distinctly half-hearted. And then, for no particular reason, he had an impression of a nurse's cap, an expanse of black hair parted in the middle, two large grey eyes that were faintly mocking. Sister Murgatroyd was bending over the divan tucking in the non-existent sheets and blankets; he closed his eyes and his arms closed tightly round Hilda.

As he dressed he felt that her contempt was less than it had been before. Though she still didn't smile or speak, except to answer his half-hearted conversation with grunts and shrugs. He thanked her and offered her a cigarette. When he got back to the waiting-room, he glanced at his watch and saw that his second tiddly-wink still had five minutes to go. It was another ten minutes before Captain Slythe reappeared, and while Sheldon was waiting for him Hilda suddenly reappeared in the doorway holding his gaiters.

'Anklets, web!' Hilda said, pronouncing the words very carefully. They were the first and last words he had heard her say. She handed him the gaiters and disappeared. As he put them on he wondered about the circumstances in which she had learned to call them by their official army designation. Was this an article of apparel that officers were always leaving behind in her room? Or did she number among her regular clients some quartermaster who, by way of cosy small-talk, taught her the correct army names of things? Had she, he wondered, ever had occasion to come to the waiting-room and say, 'Your drawers, cellular?' The thought struck him that anywhere but in bed Hilda might turn out to be great fun.

These musings were cut short by the return of Captain Slythe. He was as seedy-looking as ever, but in an unaccountable way he looked 'new': like a man who has had a haircut. He had had five minutes more than his strict allotment of time. He apologised for being late.

'That's what I like about Stella,' he added. 'She isn't a clock-watcher. How did you get on with Hilda?'

'To be honest, Slythe, this isn't quite in my line.'

'Aha. The romantic type!'

Slythe had duties at ten and said he could run Sheldon back to the hospital if he didn't mind getting back early. On the way Sheldon asked him what could be done about transport. Slythe said it wasn't too easy, but if he had some warning he might be able to help, he'd do his best. He pulled up by a side door of the hospital.

'The entrance is round the corner – but this'll do fine.'

'Sorry. Force of habit. This is the one they use when they're after time. Supposed to be in by midnight, and all that. This is a useful door to know. Dark, always open, never anyone about.'

Sheldon laughed: Slythe was unbeatable. He hoped he would never meet him after the war, he knew he wouldn't like him. War makes it possible to be fond of the most extraordinary people. That, come to think of it, was what these comradeship people went on about really meant: managing to put up with people with whom you have nothing in common.

He managed to contrive a meeting with Sister Murgatroyd in one of the corridors the next morning.

'You shouldn't be up so early,' she said. 'Has anyone taken your temperature?'

'I wanted to save you all trouble. Anyway, it's normal. Or was until I saw you.'

'I'm not in the mood. I warn you. Put your tongue out.'

He did so, pulling a slight face.

'I thought so,' she said. 'You're to take it easy today.'

'If you'd come out with me you could keep an eye on me. As it is I have to console myself the best way I can.'

'I'm telling you for your own good. Don't overdo the drinking until you are properly better.'

'Yes, ma'am! You're charming when you bully.'

'You're the first who has ever thought that. Most of them call it nagging and hate me for it.'

'It's only nagging after marriage. Before, it's bullying and it's nice when it is done by someone as attractive.'

'I warned you I wasn't in the mood. I had one hour's sleep last night.'

'I'm sorry.'

'By the way, you probably won't be with us much longer. They're going to kick out as many convalescents as possible to make room.'

'How soon is it likely to be?'

'For you, two or three days, I should say. You never know for certain. They're in rather a flap. This flood of customers caught them on the hop.'

'What happens then?'

'You go to the new convalescent centre. If it's ready, that is. About fifty miles away, in the hills. It's due to start up any time now. A glorified country club. And the ladies of the American Red Cross for company. They're running it.'

'Too far away. I shan't go.'

'The alternative is the Reinforcement Depot and a week or so of light duties. By the way, I can do tomorrow night, if you still want to take me out: if you haven't found something better.'

'You make me the happiest –' he began. But she was already away up the corridor, and he thought how remarkable it was that a girl who had done two days of this kind of hard labour with practically no sleep could look so fresh and tranquil and carry herself without a trace of fatigue.

He watched her disappear, enjoying her movements, then he made his way below and into the street where he thumbed a lift into the town.

Sheldon spent most of the morning studying the shops. He wanted to buy something for Sister Murgatroyd but he had no idea what. He hoped that by looking in shop windows he might come upon something better than the conventional trinkets, cosmetics, and well-meaning monstrosities with which vagrant soldiery usually loaded up its unfortunate womenfolk. The odd thing was that he found it impossible to connect her with civilian clothes. He saw a great many dresses, hats, shoes, nightdresses, underclothes, but he could never imagine Sister Murgatroyd in any of them. He couldn't for the life of him picture her as anything but a nurse; couldn't make even a guess at what she might wear when not in uniform. Her uniform and herself seemed an integral part of one another.

So, deciding to postpone the matter until he had given it further thought, he made for the Officers' Club, an establishment he was already beginning to find depressing – but which was rendered irresistible by the duty-free prices of drinks and cigarettes. After lunching there he spent the afternoon in a cinema.

There was a café quite close to the cinema, and about half-past five Sheldon sat down in the warm sunshine and ordered himself an anisette. For some time he was the only customer, and he was nearing the end of his second drink when a French lieutenant sat down a couple of tables away.

'Good evening,' Sheldon said. 'Would you care to join me.'

'Thank you.'

'What will you have?'

'Thank you, an anisette.'

It was some time later that Sheldon happened to mention that he had been the previous evening to Chez Suzy.

The Frenchman, whose name was Brassart, laughed.

'This is a terrible place,' he said. 'You must forgive me – it is what we call *pour les Anglais et les Américains.*'

'I'm not surprised,' Sheldon said.

'It is a joke, this Chez Suzy.'

Now if Sheldon was interested in that sort of thing, Lieutenant Brassart went on to say, he would only be too happy to take him somewhere that was really good. Had he heard of the dancers of the Oulad Naïl? No? It would be Brassart's great pleasure to show them to him. But first they must eat. One could not make love on an empty stomach: he knew a place...

The restaurant, which was in a basement, would have been impossible to find without a guide. After they had gentled their way through a meal consisting of soup, omelette, kidneys served in flaming brandy, cheese, and fruit – along with a bottle of Volnay – Brassart apologised because there hadn't been a meat course. Meat was at present impossible to get, he said. Sheldon said it was the best meal he had had during the war, and meant it. Brassart insisted that it wasn't bad for what it was: these people had to make the best of what they got, mostly scraps.

Over the brandy Sheldon learned a little more of the Oulad Naïl. They came, it seemed, from a special Berber tribe who lived in the mountain range of that name, which you had to cross to reach the northern fringes of the Sahara. The tribe were immensely proud of their dancing tradition and of the fame of their girls which had spread throughout North Africa. Many judges considered them to be the best of their kind anywhere. Only the loveliest and most talented were allowed by the tribe to go out to the dancing troupes. They had a privileged position, these girls, something like that of the hetaerae of ancient Greece; and though they were Moslems, the esteem in which they were held by their own people was in no way impaired by that part of their vocation which was not concerned with dancing. Queues of potential husbands were willing, like

Barkis, when the girls were ready to retire.

They walked through a maze of alleys in the area of the *kasbah* till eventually they came to a dark doorway in a narrow street. Brassart led the way in. They walked along a passage which led on to a courtyard, and on the far side of it there was another door. Sheldon was surprised to find how clean and cool it was inside.

A middle-aged woman approached. She was heavily made-up and jewelled, and wore Arab dress. But she had that pert trollop look which is international, and Sheldon instinctively wanted to call her Flossie. Nor would he have been surprised had she addressed him as Ducks. A spirited conversation took place between her and the Frenchman, and after some time a sum of money was agreed upon. She then led the way to a long, narrow room whose whitewashed walls and flagged floors were almost entirely covered by carpets of the most brilliant hues and by red-and-white striped rugs. Benches had been arranged round the walls to make a continuous uneven seat, and this, too, was covered with carpets.

They sat down on the ledge at one end of the room; at the other end there was a small stage on which stood the three-man band. The four girls sat cross-legged on the floor in front of the band, smoking and chattering. The room was dimly lit, the air heavy with smoke and perfume.

The band consisted of an ordinary large drum suspended from the neck of a very old man; a second drum – a hollow skin affair like an outsize tambourine – struck with the hands; and a straight, black, reed instrument with a tonal quality something like an oboe, but coarser, and much intenser in volume.

When they began to play the wild, shrill music of endlessly repeated half-tones, quarter-tones, trills, and wails, there was at times the effect of bagpipes; but the music, when your ear had attuned itself to harmonic shades that do not exist in Western music – with the pounding rhythm of the drums to sustain it – was perceived to have a form of its own, a form much more complex than the simple wail of the Scottish folk music. It was unearthly and primitive and without apparent beginning or end: yet it had a form once you had adjusted yourself to it. So, at any rate, it seemed to Sheldon.

The four girls, in shapeless low-waisted dresses of different colours, put down their cigarettes, rose casually to their feet, and slithered into their dance.

The main features of it were a phenomenal upward flicking of the belly rapidly in time with the music and the movement of their feet; and a sliding of the head from side to side of the shoulders, a smooth rhythmic movement in which the head always remained vertical, yet moved almost across the full width of the shoulders. The third speciality was vocal. Periodically they would hit a high, tearing top note and at the same time slap their open mouths with cupped hands to produce a shrieking, barbaric trill. This seemed to be a sort of signature tune, and they repeated it at regular intervals. To emphasise the belly motion they constantly pushed their girdles below their hips as they danced.

When they had completed this opening ensemble – in which the main elements of their dancing were introduced – they slouched back to their seat along the wall near the stage and picked up the cigarettes which they had left burning in an ashtray. Then each girl came out in turn and gave a solo consisting of variations on the basic movements of belly and head. One did it with a vase balanced on her head. Another broke suddenly – in the middle of her dance – into a wailing chant that sounded like a groan of despair. Another added more elaborate dance steps. They continued in this way for about half an hour. First the whole group, then the solo variations, then the group again.

The anisette was taking its delayed-action effect, and Sheldon felt strangely excited. He was surprised, too, that the girls were as lovely as they were. They were quite different and each was a beauty. Their skin was a pale golden-bronze and had the texture and consistency of cream. Their faces were perfectly formed as well as beautiful. The one Sheldon liked best was one who reminded him of a young, naughty Mona Lisa. Her face tapered from high cheekbones, and the hint of naughtiness came from a wicked little upturned mouth, and from the eyes – through the heavily blacked lashes they appeared to be fawn – which seemed to contain some childish secret.

When, after half an hour, the dancing stopped the musicians left the stage and the girls stepped onto it, drawing the curtains across.

'They now take their clothes off,' the Frenchman said. 'Then they will do the same dances, but without the belly movement which they do not make without their clothes.'

The musicians then did a strange thing. They went to the door and huddled between it and the curtain which hung down it – so that they were partially hidden from the room. But as they took their instruments into hiding with them, it was necessary for them to bend forward and thrust the curtain well clear of the door with their backsides. In this position they began to play, the bulging curtain heaving and shaking grotesquely as their backsides moved beneath it in time with the music they were pouring into the door.

The girls darted through the stage curtains in turn and danced round the room performing the same solos as before, except for the belly flick, and now they were naked except for the chains of gold coins they wore around their necks. All trace of hair had been removed from the golden-bronze bodies which were rounded but slim: surprisingly slim after you had seen them in those shapeless dresses.

After the last girl had finished her solo and disappeared behind the stage curtains, the band emerged, panting and apparently much relieved, from their cramped bending posture behind the curtain on the door. The curtains on the stage were drawn, and the girls, clothed again, stepped into the room for a final ensemble. The band played its way back to the stage for a final flare-up of still wilder and louder sound; the girls danced their final steps, tapping their mouths almost continuously to produce the effect of demented, trilling furies; then the dance stopped rather than ended, and the girls slouched back to their seat as casually as they had left it in the first place.

It was as formal as classical ballet, with Eastern casualness in place of Western discipline; but the very artlessness of it enhanced its sense of primitive excitement.

Lieutenant Brassart and the Bedouin Flossie went into a protracted bargaining engagement – apparently still necessary though agreement had been reached before the performance. At the end of it he handed her 2500 francs which she accepted with a deprecating shrug, as though she were letting him off more lightly than he knew.

'Do you wish to continue?' Brassart then said.

'It would be an abuse of your hospitality not to,' Sheldon said.

It was more of a cell than a room. A queer little lop-sided cell with an arched ceiling and walls that were neither straight nor parallel. It was lit by a single small oil lamp. There was a heap of rugs on the floor, and a red and white striped one on top. The naughty Mona Lisa was lying on the rugs. She was naked and she was smoking an American cigarette. As soon as he was inside the room she sat up and smiled.

As he sat beside her on the rugs his leg began to ache. A steady throb reminded him that he was still a *pauvre blessé*. He pointed to the bandage and made motions and faces to indicate a state of tenderness, but she merely giggled, and the more he tried to make her understand his French the more she giggled; then, without warning, she flung her arms round him, welded her lips onto his, and with her nails and the tips of her strong fingers she began to probe and feel for the secret spring of his back, and soon he was unaware of his aching leg, unaware of anything but an ecstasy, wild beyond imagining. He loved her on into the night. Whenever he lay beside her stroking the cream-smooth hairless skin he knew this was the most perfectly formed face he had ever seen or would see, this was perfection. When finally he lay thus at her side, tired and a little sad from loving, and she turned the light-brown eyes on to his, he looked into them, wondering; stared into their heartless innocence and felt afraid. There was a purity in this face to inspire fear as well as ecstasy: the barbaric inhuman purity of being for whom right and wrong do not exist.

It was after ten when they left the house, they had been there nearly three hours.

'How much did you give her?' Brassart asked.

'Three thousand.'

'Too much,' the Frenchman said in a practical tone of voice.

They were winding back through the alleys and side streets and Sheldon wondered how the other remembered the way. All of a sudden they burst into a main street, and Sheldon saw that they were near the club.

'Let's have a drink.'

'That would be nice,' Brassart said.

'Tell me,' said Sheldon. 'Why did the band go behind the door curtain when the girls danced in the nude?'

'As Moslems they must not look at a naked woman in public.'

'In those particular circumstances it seems a bit peculiar.'

'It is their custom. Though upstairs they can be with the girls like anyone else. As a matter of fact the younger of the drummers is the boyfriend of the girl you were with.'

'Good God!' Sheldon said. 'Doesn't he mind?'

'No. To be engaged to one of the Oulad Naïl is considered by these people a great honour. When she is too old to dance she will marry him.'

'When is that likely to be?'

'Oh. Usually when they are about eighteen. They aren't much good after that.'

'Eighteen! My little girl looks that now. They all did for that matter. They didn't strike me as ageing.'

'That little girl you were with is not yet fourteen. I happen to know.'

At the club a man said he could give Sheldon a lift back to the hospital as long as he didn't mind waiting a little: Brassart was billeted in the town and had no transport problem. They ordered drinks and sat down. Two grey-clad army nurses walked past on their way out of the club. Seeing them reminded Sheldon abruptly of Sister Murgatroyd: he realised he hadn't thought of her all evening. He felt curiously guilty about this.

'Why,' Brassart wanted to know, 'do English nurses always have a moustache?'

'They don't,' Sheldon said. 'You are libelling the English rose.'

'I love the English rose. I love her always except when she is on a bicycle and when she has a moustache.'

'Some of our nurses are lovely,' Sheldon said. He was rather drunk now. 'Very lovely. Some of them. Believe you me, *mon ami*. Oh, God, I'm tired. This night life is killing me.'

'I think your chauffeur is ready,' Brassart said. The man who had offered him a lift was walking over. He nearly fell asleep during the ride, and by the time he had climbed the hospital stairs he was dead tired.

During the last few days he had walked past the Sisters' office many times in the hope of catching Sister Murgatroyd in it. Tonight he found himself tip-toeing past it as quickly as possible so as not to be caught by her in his present state. His course along the passage was a little unsteady, but he reached the ward undetected and got himself into bed without undue commotion.

'You won't get any sympathy from me,' she said, planting the breakfast tray before him.

'Oh, Sister, I feel awful.'

'And I've news for you. You're being discharged tomorrow.'

'Tomorrow! It's a bit sudden, isn't it?'

'I don't see why you should care. You've practically discharged yourself already.'

She was scolding with the conventional primness of her calling, but there was a smiling mockery in her eyes. Eventually he managed to discern this in spite of his hang-over, his tiredness, and his aching leg. She had him at her mercy and she was enjoying herself. She even left him for three minutes with a thermometer in his mouth.

'This changes things a bit,' he said, when she came back to liberate his mouth. 'Any chance of your coming out tomorrow as well as tonight?'

'Afraid not,' she said. They both spoke now in jerky whispers so that the others in the ward could not overhear.

'Tomorrow, then,' he said. 'Final celebration of my release from this damn gaol.'

'Tomorrow would be best for me.'

'Fine. Aren't you free at all today?'

'Only this afternoon. I was going into Algiers for an hour to shop.

We've a truck going in.'

'Room for me?'

'All right then. It'll be just there and back. The truck won't wait. Might be time for a cup of tea.'

'Where will I pick you up?'

'Outside the Sisters' mess – two-thirty.'

So tomorrow they would throw him out! Now that it was imminent the thought of going to the Reinforcement Depot filled him with repugnance. A week or two of light duties and then they'd send him off in charge of a draft of odds-and-sods, and they'd spend a week getting to the front, and he himself would probably end up with another unit. On the spur of the moment he decided he would hitch-hike back to the Battalion, by air if he could wangle it. Tomorrow he would take Sister Murgatroyd off somewhere for the night. The day after he would report not to the Reinforcement Centre but to the airport. Technically he would be a deserter. But there was a certain amount of *panache* about deserting *to* the front. He began to feel quite homesick for the Battalion. The Battalion was where he lived, where he belonged. Now that the hospital was finishing with him there was only one thing to do – to get back to the Battalion as quickly as possible. But he must get hold of Slythe. There were certain administrative aspects of his plans that needed the assistance of the resourceful captain. When Sheldon telephoned him he offered to drive over to the hospital.

'Can't understand you hero types,' Captain Slythe said sadly. 'Chance to kick around a reinforcement place for a week or two doing sweet F.A. and you bust yourself to go back and get killed. Can't understand it at all. What do you want me to do?'

'I've got a special date tomorrow night. A very special date, you understand? I want somewhere quiet to go: a means of getting there and of course a means of getting back the next day, that is the day after tomorrow.'

Captain Slythe thought hard.

'I'd lend you a vehicle like a shot. Can't though. They've got very stuffy about that sort of thing lately. How will this do? There's a small place about ten miles up the coast – St. Julien. One of my ration lorries goes through it every evening, leaving Algiers at seven. Same fellow drives back the next morning, reaching St. Julien about nine-thirty. There's a pub of sorts at St. Julien: more of a café, I suppose you'd call it. But the old girl has a room she doesn't mind letting. She's very fond of Spam, for some reason, and Chesterfields. It helps to have a good supply, you'll find.'

'Slythe, you're wonderful. What's the name of the café, by the way?'

'Damned if I remember. But it's the only one. You can't miss it.'

'Where'll I pick up your man?'

'Better make it outside the Aletti. Tomorrow evening at seven. The driver's name is Thompson. Driver Thompson, incidentally, is very partial to whisky and obviously can't afford it on his pay. It would do no harm at all to have a little on you.'

'Splendid. Many thanks. Oh, there's one other thing. I want to get on a plane the day after tomorrow.'

'Shouldn't be any difficulty. Tell you what, when you come back from St. Julien come right back to our place on the lorry. I can run you up to the airfield. I know the R.A.F. fellow who runs the transport end. He'll fix something.'

'I repeat, you're wonderful.'

'I do no more than my duty,' Slythe said. 'It's the function of the Service Corps to service the fighting troops.'

By the time Sister Murgatroyd had finished her shopping they had barely twenty minutes for tea.

'I've been active since I last saw you. What happens if you're not back in hospital by midnight?'

'Nothing, if I'm not on duty.'

'You mean you just have to be back in time for next day's duty?'

'Of course.'

'So theoretically you could stay out all night?'

'Of course. We sometimes do, when the duties work out right. We stay at the Y.W.C.A. We try to work it so that a night off and a morning off occasionally go together so that we can have a complete break away from the place.'

'What time are you on duty the day after tomorrow?'

'Two in the afternoon.'

'Tomorrow night you will be sleeping at the Y.W.C.A. in St. Julien.'

'Where is St. Julien?'

'A few miles up the coast. We're dining there tomorrow, you and I.'

'Why the Y.W.C.A.?'

'Because the bus services are bad and I don't want us to have to hurry over our meal. In case I don't see you again will you meet me outside the Aletti at seven sharp? We're being picked up there.'

'What about your reinforcement place?'

'I've decided not to go.'

'Decided not to go! Just like that?'

'Just like that. I've decided that my career must come first. Tell you about it later. Now about tomorrow – '

The lorry detached itself from the traffic streaming past the Aletti Hotel and pulled into the side.

'Major Sheldon, I presume?'

'Driver Thompson, I suppose. Good evening. We'll get in the back.'

He helped her in and as the lorry started up he fished around until he found a loose tarpaulin among the piles of ration boxes. This he folded and laid out as a mattress, and, after much heaving and shifting of the cargo of boxes, he managed to make a corridor wide enough to enable them to sit side by side, with their backs against the hard wooden end behind the driver's cab. It is the least uncomfortable way in which to travel *à deux* in a three-ton ration lorry, he informed her.

She wore the drab, grey overcoat that went with the nurse's uniform. She was in uniform because the sight of a civilian woman in an army lorry would have drawn suspicious glances: whereas in these parts at this time a nurse was taken for granted in any situation.

'At last, at last,' he said.

'And Pullman comfort,' she said, squirming. 'This thing across my back is hard.'

'Best I could manage. The Daimler was busy.'

'You've been very clever, actually. You've learned your way around fast.'

'You smell nice.'

'How delicately you put it. It's Lelong.'

'It suits you better than ether. I suppose a man gave it you.'

'Yes.'

'What man?'

'Just a man. Man with a bullet in his leg like you. A better leg than yours, though. A lovely leg, it was.'

'D'you specialise in leg wounds?'

'Yes. You can keep them in order better. They can't run so fast.'

He put his arm through hers and squeezed. With the hand of the other he twisted a packet of cigarettes out of his pocket, lit one and handed it to her, lighting a second for himself. They sat close together smoking contentedly and in silence as the lorry, changing gear frequently in the congestion of the central town, flung them first to one side and then to the other in their slot between the stacked, rattling ration boxes.

It was the first time he had seen her smoke. She smoked, as some women do, in a slow deliberate way, as though every puff were a major event. She drew the smoke in deeply, hollowing her cheeks as she did so. Then she would blow it out again in a very fine jet, just as deliberately. This manner of smoking had always rather irritated him, affecting him much in the same way as the elevated little finger of the prissy tea-drinker. It was the first time she had made any movement that wasn't, as far as he was concerned, completely graceful. How damaging were tiny prejudices!

'I hope your leg isn't being shaken up too badly.'

'I've never been more comfortable,' he said and tightened his arm around her waist. What the hell did the smoking matter! What a stupid tetchy idiot he must be turning into. This was wonderful, quite wonderful; his cheek was against hers and her rough, grey, hideous nurse's coat rubbed against his neck, and it didn't matter, it didn't spoil anything.

When the lorry dropped them at St. Julien they stepped straight onto the beach and sniffed the sea. It was a dark night; there was no moon and the sky was overcast, but it was very fresh and not too cold. She took off her coat and took several deep breaths. That, too, she did deliberately and with her head held high so that it seemed important: it was a great quality of hers, Sheldon thought, this ability to make commonplace actions important. It was a part of that sense of style. She seemed suddenly happy and released standing there in the darkness, her head held high, staring out to sea and breathing the air deeply, and he knew better than to break in on her thoughts. Then she turned away from it with a little sigh.

'I love the sea,' she said. 'I'm rather silly about it.'

Sheldon took her by the hands and faced her.

'I have a terrible confession to make,' he said. 'There is no Y.W.C.A in St. Julien.'

'I too have a terrible confession to make,' she said. 'I know.'

He kissed her hard then, hard and long, and she kissed back but not so hard.

'You wait here,' he said, 'and have a bit more sea while I take our bags and get things organised where we're going to stay. I'll be back as soon as I have arranged everything.'

The Grand Café de Provence turned out to be less impressive than its name: a sort of glorified beach hut with an upper storey. The café itself contained five small tables which looked as though no one had sat at them for years. The room was lit by a single yellow electric bulb which hung naked and clouded from a length of dusty flex. A short square woman appeared from the back.

'*Bon soir!*' Sheldon said with a bright ingratiating smile. '*Je suis le bon ami de Capitaine Slythe.*'

'*Qui?*' she snapped.

'*Capitaine Slythe. De l'armée Britannique,*' he added, narrowing the field.

'*Capitaine Slythe? Qui?*' she snapped.

'*Je veux une chambre à deux personnes, s'il vous plaît.*'

'*Venez!*' she barked and led him up an unsafe stairway to a glorified loft containing a double bed, a broken chair, a small table, and a wash-bowl. '*Cinq cent francs chaque personne.*'

'Oh, God!' Sheldon muttered.

'*Quoi?*'

'*D'accord. Je cherche Madame. Nous voulons aussi du dîner.*'

'*Oh-o-o-o,*' she said with a cosmic shrug of derision. '*Du dîner! Presque rien – pas de viande, pas des légumes, pas de –*'

'*Un moment!*' he broke in, fishing inside his haversack. He passed her two tins each of Spam and stew. Two, he gave her to understand, were for her, the others for their dinner, augmented by whatever she could provide in addition. Her manner mellowed, but grudgingly, so he gave her a packet of Chesterfields to ease her along. This softened her to the extent of a half-hearted promise to see what she could do in the matter of dinner; but things were difficult, one knew how it was, this terrible war – and she was off again.

She was standing where he had left her. She was still gazing out to sea and he loved her simple dignity and repose and stopped for a moment to enjoy the sight of her. She stood very still and she seemed to be a part of the night. He kissed her, and her cheeks and the tip of her nose were cold now from the night air.

'How did you get on?'

'I'm afraid it isn't the Ritz.'

'I didn't expect that it would be.'

'Actually,' he said uncomfortably, 'it's – it's a bit rough. I hope you won't hate it too much. At least it's quiet.'

'That's good,' she said.

'A horrible old witch runs it, but she softened up a bit when I produced the goodies. You often get amazingly good meals in that sort of place.'

'You're brilliant,' she said. 'Let's go.' He took her in his arms and covered her with kisses. He kissed the white front of her cap, then the hair below it; he kissed each temple in turn, kissed the cold tip of her nose, kissed her on the mouth and held her very tight and felt the starched front of her apron crinkle against him and he held her tighter, kissing her until she broke from him breathless.

'Darling, Sister,' he said, 'I love you, I love you, I love you.'

'My name is Mary and I don't believe a word.'

'To me you are Sister Murgatroyd. There are thousands of Marys but only one Sister Murgatroyd. You are unique and quite beautiful, and I love you.' She took his hand and started walking towards the café.

While she changed – she was unexpectedly offered the use of the old woman's own room, which had a basin with running water – Sheldon waited in the café, helping himself freely to the gin he had brought with him and feeling very happy. It was a wonderful night. She was the most wonderful person in the world. Life was wonderful. Everything was wonderful. Then she appeared.

She had changed into a rather shapeless dress of flowered cotton and over it wore a brown cardigan which was loosely buttoned. Her hair, which he had never before seen without the nurse's cap, was limp and lustreless and it was drawn carelessly at the back into a wispy bun. She wore no stockings, just an old pair of white gym shoes which made her feet seem unusually broad. She was smiling.

He poured out two large drinks. She gulped hers quickly and handed him her glass for another. She began to talk in an easy relaxed manner he had never known in her before. And for the first time he heard her laugh. The effect was upsetting: when she laughed the poise and the style he had loved in her vanished. There are women, he thought, who should laugh often and those who should never laugh, and she was in the second category. Unexpectedly it was more of a giggle than a laugh, and the more she drank the more frequent it became; not because she was getting drunk but simply because she was utterly relaxed. She told him about herself with an easy abandon of which he had never suspected her capable: of her childhood in Bexleyheath, of her father who worked for an insurance company, of her days with an amateur dramatic society, of her hospital training. With growing dismay he realised that Sister Murgatroyd, the diva of the wards, had turned into Mary Murgatroyd of Bexleyheath: a giggling graceless Englishwoman on holiday and letting herself go.

He hated himself for having these thoughts and tried to drown them with more gin, but though he fought them hard they refused to be entirely suppressed. He searched desperately in his mind for something specially nice to say to her but it was no good. The magic had gone out of something. The drink was beginning to go to her head now, and she continued to chatter and giggle a great deal. Had she really changed or was it just him?

The meal was terrible. The tinned meat he had brought had been liquefied into a greasy, brown mess, and this had been slopped onto some poor-grade rice to make what the old woman described as a Pilaf Spécial. Sheldon kept apologising for it, and they made up for it with fruit: that, at least, was plentiful and good. Throughout the meal and after she continued to talk and to laugh happily, saying she hadn't had such fun for years; it was her first party since coming abroad; it was wonderful to relax just for once and forget all about being a Lady with a Lamp.

After they had drunk their coffee and two glasses of brandy she sighed contentedly and said she was deliciously tired.

'It's a lovely night,' he said, 'let us take the brandy bottle outside.' He poured out two large measures. On top of the other drinks he had had the brandy was making him quite drunk, but he noticed that it did not seem to affect her. She had developed a flush and her nose had become shiny, but apart from that she seemed able to lap it up indefinitely without its having any effect on her. He felt vaguely resentful of this.

'I'm so tired,' she said again.

'One for th'road,' he said firmly.

When they had drunk that one, she yawned and said: 'I think we've both had enough.'

'Binder!' he said. 'Mus' have binder. Pity to leave this little bit in the bottle.'

He woke up with a start to see that she was already dressed. She was making up her lips in a small hand-mirror. His head throbbed dreadfully.

'You've half an hour,' she said. 'I thought I'd get myself done and leave you a clear field.'

'God, I feel awful.'

'I'm not surprised. To tell the truth I'm not feeling so wonderful myself.'

'You look extremely fresh,' he grumbled. 'God, I feel awful.'

'You'll feel better when you've put your head under the tap and tasted some air. I should use the kitchen sink.'

He groped for a cigarette, lit it, and began to cough violently.

'I don't wish to sound beastly,' she said. 'But the lorry is due to pick us up in twenty-five minutes. You really will feel better when you have washed.'

The lorry travelled much faster on the way back. The ration boxes were empty on the return journey and this made the load much lighter. Every jolt, every lurch made Sheldon's head ache.

'What happened?' he suddenly demanded. 'I remember sitting out there drinking brandy. But I can't remember what happened after.'

'Oh, nothing,' she said. 'We just went to bed.'

'I must have been very tight.'

'Just a little.'

'It's a wonder I got up those stairs to that damned loft where we slept.'

'It certainly is.'

'Was I difficult?'

'No. Not really. It was all right once I'd got you past the old woman's door.'

'Oh, Lord! What did I do?'

'You wanted to go in and tell her that her cooking stank – that was the word you used; kept using, in fact. You're heavier than you look.'

The lorry lurched. A hammer pounded his brain. He looked at her miserably.

'You carried me upstairs?'

'More or less.' She was smiling.

'Oh dear. It must have nearly killed you.'

'You were rather heavier than I expected. But I was so relieved to get you away from the old lady's door.'

He lay silent for a while, his aching head resting on her shoulder, the hammer continuing to pound his brain extra hard whenever the lorry struck a rough patch of road, which was constantly.

'I've just thought of something,' he said. 'You must have undressed me, too.'

'That was the easiest part,' she said. 'Nurses are used to it. Though you were a little bit coy to begin with. You giggled and said I was tickling. Then you went right off to sleep and slept like a baby. Except that you snored rather dreadfully.'

'I'm sorry,' he said. 'Sorry as hell. I must be out of practice. By the way, I'm flying back to the Battalion this afternoon.'

'I know. You told me at least a dozen times.'

'I told you that, too?'

The lorry pulled up and the muffled voice of Driver Thompson announced from the cab that they had reached the hospital.

'It was great fun,' she said. 'Many, many thanks, Tim.'

'Dear Mary,' he said, 'thank you. And sorry again for –'

'Nothing. I enjoyed it enormously. The very best of luck, my dear. And be careful with that leg.'

She kissed him quickly on the forehead and jumped out of the lorry. He climbed down after her but she was already hurrying through the hospital gate: though not so much hurrying, he thought, as covering the ground quickly without hurrying. The way she moved about the wards and corridors of the hospital. Not Mary Murgatroyd of Bexleyheath, but the queenly Sister Murgatroyd.

He climbed into the cab alongside Driver Thompson and the air through the open windscreen was a great comfort.

At Maison Blanche airfield Slythe drove straight through to a hut marked 'Wing-Commander J. C. Bristol – Private'. He entered without knocking, beckoning to Sheldon to follow.

'Hello, Dolly,' Slythe said. 'Hero type here wants a lift to the war. Can do?'

'Hiya,' said the wing-commander. 'Let me see. Mind travelling with a lot of boxes?'

'I'm getting very used to it,' Sheldon said.

'There's a Dakota leaving in twenty minutes with a load of stores.' He scribbled rapidly on a slip of paper. 'Show this at Passenger Control.'

'It's very good of you.'

'A pleasure. Better get over there soon, they'll be leaving on time.'

'I don't know what I would have done without you,' he said to Slythe.

'It was nothing. See you again one of these days.'

'Hope so. Thanks again for everything.'

'By the way, how did last night go?'

'Oh, fine.'

As the aircraft climbed and he made himself a bed of yellow life-saving equipment between the pile of ammunition boxes and the side of the cabin, he felt suddenly glad that he was going back. There is a psychological time when you know something has ended, and Being Wounded had now ended. It had been an interlude of unreality, a fantasy, a mad incredible honeymoon. Now he wanted impatiently to get back to the Battalion. For better or for worse that was where his war was, where he had grown used to its being. Not that he wanted to fight again: he wasn't thirsting for action. It was simply that it seemed the most natural thing to do: to go back where you belonged. The Battalion was where he belonged. It was his whole existence. He wanted badly now to be back there with those of whom he had become so much a part and who had become so much a part of him. For him there could only be the Battalion. Now it was tugging at him umbilically and he was glad. Lying alone in the cargo-laden body of the plane he found that already his experiences as a *pauvre blessé* were dissolving into a jumble of confused impressions, like the events of a long night recollected through a hang-over. Already it was becoming difficult to believe that much of it really happened. The delirium, the intermission of suspended time, had ended. It had been mad and marvellous, and now it seemed untrue.

At Souk el Arba, which they reached in less than two hours,

he found a truck leaving for the headquarters of his division, from which transport to his unit would be easy to procure. So he arrived at the Battalion shortly before midnight, coming up with the rations. Nothing was very changed. They were still in the same place. A few people were missing. Jimmie Morton had become C.O. and his hair was going grey although he was only twenty-seven. That more than anything pressed home the realisation that he was back. The holiday was over: was as dead as if it had never happened. More than ever he began to wonder if it had. He was back... back...

SIX

THAT HAD BEEN so many, so very many, weeks ago. Being wounded was something in the past, something remote and long ago. Since then there had been, interminably, the fierce little winter battles that are no less dreadful than the large ones, though they only come to be known in jargon phrases: consolidating our gains, certain readjustment of our positions, local activity, defensive aggression, and all the rest of them. But they were real enough if you were in them. The long, wasting fight against the winter: the wet, the cold, the boredom of days when nothing happened except the shelling. The casual, even lazy shelling which always, however, picked off one or two. You tried to read, you couldn't concentrate; you tried to write, you couldn't concentrate; you were aware of spiritual atrophy and powerless to resist it.

The long winter nights, cold with dread, when every sound is a tensing threat, and behind the hills – your hills and theirs – the guns thrash the dark with a St. Vitus's dance of light. If you go back and watch them from close quarters you see that they have beauty, those great guns, as they rear with the agony of recoil, and the flame-spit licks juicily round the lips of the muzzle: beauty they have as well as terror. And the patrols, the long sweeping patrols deep into the night. Once – perhaps, in the dim long ago when you were fresh, there was in some of them the elemental exhilaration of the hunt: the pitting of animal wits against animal wits in the dark: the skilful mastery of ground to make the silent stealthy approach, the seeing without being seen.

As Sheldon reached his Company at the end of the long descent from Piecrust, his batman met him and handed him half a mug of tea.

'Only half?' he said.

'Yes, sir. They're not back from the water point yet. They shouldn't be long. There will be more later.'

When he had drunk the tea he still had a few minutes before he was due to brief the patrol. He examined the blister on his right foot and found that it had not developed sufficiently to be pricked. He would have to soap his sock well and hope for the best. He didn't like putting plaster on them at that stage, the plaster always crinkled and then you were worse off than if there were none.

Sitting outside his dugout – a hole scooped out of the bank at the bottom of the Charlie Company hill – he could see most of his depleted Company, and it had never seemed to him so small. Over on the right was old Ainsworth, his second-in-command, reading as usual his *Pickwick* and chuckling whenever it reached his favourite bits. Strange chap, Ainsworth. A stubborn Yorkshire schoolmaster, quite without charm. Yet he had turned himself into a good officer by sheer persistence and hard work. He did all the things a junior officer was supposed to do: he saw that his men's kit was always in good order; he scrounged things for them: he went to endless trouble in their interest. Yet they couldn't like him because he was intrinsically unlikeable. But they recognised his worth. It doesn't say so in the books, but an officer ought to have charm. It is more important than good administration. It is the first requirement.

Over on the left he saw the new subaltern, Brooks. He was talking with three or four of his men. They seemed to be getting along easily enough. No self-consciousness on either side. Brooks was all right. He'd soon learn the form. A company commander, Sheldon thought, is a sort of match-maker when he posts a new officer to a platoon. That one was going to be a good marriage. You could always tell. Brooks was all right. He had charm. Poor Ainsworth. Without charm your administration had to be so *bloody* good. And still they didn't *like* you. Only admired.

It was slightly reassuring, after the depressing afternoon on Piecrust, to look round the battered little Company and watch the familiar faces just being themselves. The Sergeant-Major, gossiping away as usual, fourteen to the dozen. A tiger in times of 'real soldiering', he seemed to shrink in circumstances where dress, blanco and drill had ceased to matter. He had turned into a tetchy garrulous nanny, who was still somewhat redundant on hand after the children had grown up and started to live their own lives.

With the Sergeant-Major – and as usual saying very little – was the peerless Sergeant Prince. Tall, finely proportioned, perfectly disciplined in speech, dress, and bearing – the classic sergeant of infantry. Born and orphaned in India, the Army was at once his mother and father, his upbringing, his education, his home, his way of life, his whole existence. More than once it had been suggested that he should try for a commission, but he never would – nor did he give reasons. It was as though he knew instinctively and precisely what was for him. As a platoon sergeant he was a complete master of his trade, a celebrity in his own right. In due course he could expect to become Sergeant-Major. In the meantime he did his job, the job of his choosing, the job of which he was completely the master. And he seemed happy to do so. Sheldon found the sight of Sergeant Prince more reassuring than anything that had happened all day.

He lit his pipe – a battered Dunhill with the bowl and mouthpiece held together by insulating tape – and puffed at it. Behind him, inside the dugout, Perks the batman was cleaning Sheldon's Sten gun.

'I'd like to come with you tonight, sir,' the batman said.

'No, Perks. Not tonight.'

'Why not, sir?'

'Everything's arranged. Anyway, a woman's place is in the home.'

'Like 'ell,' said Perks.

'I'd rather leave you here so you can fuss over me when I get back. You're nice to come home to.'

'Like 'ell,' said Perks, a railway ganger whose heart was larger than his vocabulary.

'You can start by seeing I get something decent to eat before I go out.'

Sergeant Prince appeared and said the men were ready. Sheldon said he'd be right over. He stepped down into the dugout and told Perks to hold up a mirror. Then he tidied himself meticulously. He combed his hair, adjusted his collar and tie, buttoned the flaps of his breast pockets, smoothed his blouse, and tightened his belt. As he stepped back into the open he put on his forage cap, setting it at a gay angle. Then he strode off – his left hand deep in his pocket, his right hand tightly gripping the pipe – to where the men were waiting.

They sat in a cluster on the hillside, about sixty yards away. Ten Pint Midgeley, the burly glass-blower from St. Helens, who was the official Company humourist; Ginger Mobbs, a redhead from the Lancashire collieries; Bilsbury, a big man, by trade an undertaker's assistant; Tubbs and Tyldesley, diminutive but wiry clerks from Liverpool who had been inseparable since their names were first called out in alphabetical succession at their very first army roll-call. The Sergeant-Major and Sergeant Prince were there too, and, as Sheldon approached, the Sergeant-Major barked: 'Pay attention to the Company Commander'. It was an automatic incantation which came out in a single bark of sound and it was unnecessary.

'The object of the patrol, as you know, is to find out whether White Farm is occupied or not. Div think they've pulled out. We will of course approach the place tonight as if it is occupied.' Sheldon paused.

'I had a look at it this afternoon from Piecrust. The main building is large and white – the only white one in that area – so it shouldn't be difficult to identify it even though we shan't have moonlight.

'The ground in front is quite open so it is a question of going in from the right or the left. The left seems to disappear into a largish wood: the right is more open except that it has a few barns and out-buildings. My guess is that the wood is likely to be strongly defended as the most likely line of approach. I intend, therefore, to go in from the right.

'My orders are to avoid a fight, if possible, but as far as I could see from Piecrust it's going to be damn difficult to get in close without being spotted. So we need to be prepared for a battle.' He put away his pipe and lit a cigarette. He had an idea he was speaking more quickly than usual.

'That's the general idea,' he said with deliberate casualness. 'Now for a few details.' He paused intentionally.

'One: action if fired on. Down at once into fire positions, but no one to open up except on my order.

'Two: withdrawal. If we have to fight our way out the method will be the usual one – short bounds with Brens automatically leap-frogging.

'If the place does turn out to be empty, we'll have a quick look round and see what we can see, then we'll clear off home. Loot – however tempting and portable – will be severely left alone. Private Midgeley to make a special note of that last order.' Midgeley grinned and the others laughed. (Thank God for Ten Pint, he's always good for a laugh.)

There were some administrative details about dress, ammunition, and rum issue, after which Sheldon sent them off to tea.

'By the way, Sergeant-Major,' he said before leaving, 'tell Battalion Headquarters we'll be testing weapons at seventeen-thirty.' It was a routine procedure to ensure that news of the weapon-firing was circulated to the other companies, so that the sudden outbreak didn't raise an alarm.

Sheldon was relieved when the briefing was over. He couldn't shake off the feeling that his manner had been different: that the men would have noticed it. But at least it was the last formal public appearance he had to make. He wished he didn't feel so edgy. Had they noticed anything? Perhaps it would be best if he went over to where they were having tea and showed himself. Showed that he was the same person by talking and joking with them. But he didn't want to see them again until the patrol. He didn't want to talk with them or with anyone else. He didn't want to have anything more to do with them until he joined them in the semi-darkness at eighteen-hundred hours, and led them silently into the night. It wouldn't be so bad then because after that there could be no talking at all except for occasional whispered orders.

All the same he found himself irresistibly drawn to where they were, and he stood by the cooks for a few minutes and managed a couple of facetious remarks to impress on them how normal everything was and how he was just the same old Sheldon. And when he left there, he saw Sergeant Prince and two soldiers carrying a number of Bren and Sten guns up the hill to test them. He hurried after them and caught up with them as the Sergeant began to loose off bursts high into the air in the direction of no man's land. There was nothing remarkable in his joining them and firing a few bursts himself. He was, after all, commanding the patrol. It was simply that this testing of the guns was a task that had always been left to Sergeant Prince, the acknowledged weapon academician of the Battalion, and this just happened to be the first occasion on which Sheldon had ever joined in. It struck the Sergeant as strange. But of course he betrayed no hint of this: in fact he gave the impression that it had made his evening to have no less a figure than the Company Commander as a guest at this important ritual.

'I bin lookin' for you everywhere, Major,' the batman grumbled when Sheldon returned to the dugout. 'I done it, sir.'

'Done what, Perks?'

'Got you some special grub, same as you asked for. A tin of steak and kidney pud.'

'What a shame; I'm not very hungry. Better have it yourself.'

'Don't be daft, sir. An army marches on its flamin' stomach, don't it? Well, eat this up and don't argue. If you knew what I had to do to get it. It must be the last tin of steak and kidney in the 'ole Brigade.'

'Perks, you're wonderful. For your sake a couple of mouthfuls. Though I don't really want it. I don't want anything. Give me a spoon, I'll eat it out of the tin.'

'That's the idea, sir.'

Sheldon ate slowly and without enjoyment. When he had eaten less than half he handed the tin back to Perks.

'The rest is yours. Tip it in your mess-tin.'

'Kit for tonight, sir?'

'Oh, yes,' Sheldon said absently. 'The usual. This suit, my other boots, cap comforter, grenade, Sten, knife, and some cocoa for my face.'

'That's what I thought, sir,' Perks said, pointing to the corner of the dugout where those items were already neatly laid out. 'All ready for you, sir. But you forgot one thing, you'll be wanting your mucky blouse, the one without flashes.'

'Oh, yes.'

On patrol they always wore clothing from which badges of identification had been removed.

'I'll have a new pair of socks, too. Have we got any left?'

'I've put some out, sir.'

'Thanks, Perks.'

'If you want me, sir, I'll be yonder.' Yonder meant anywhere within range of a shout from Sheldon. He had many virtues, this soldier, who in peacetime helped to repair railway tracks. He knew unerringly when to be familiar, when formal: when to joke, when to keep quiet. But his greatest gift was his instinctive sense of when his presence wasn't wanted. As Perks disappeared through the entrance, Sheldon, crouched in the back of the dugout, knew that from now on he was on his own. This was his show. His only. No one could help him any more.

He began to prepare himself, like an actor who has received his first call. He put on the new socks, then dipping a piece of soap into water he began to rub it hard over the ball of his blistered foot, wetting the soap and rubbing it until a frothy paste lay across the foot: a wodge of lubricant that would ease the friction between the blister and the sole of the boot. It was a trick he had been shown as a recruit before his very first route march. Almost ever since, his hardening feet had needed no such aid; he seldom had blisters, but now he had one on this of all nights and the trick he had learned in the nursery of his soldiering came back to him.

He laced up his boots but not fully tight: he would be on his feet most of the night and they would swell. He removed his shirt and put on a high-necked jersey. Then he reached for the tin lid in which cocoa powder had been watered into a thick brown paste. He began to rub this into his face and neck to darken them – you couldn't use mud round here or you picked up skin diseases – and when he had darkened his face and neck and behind the ears he rubbed the rest on the hands and wrists, and as it began to dry and his face started to itch, he thought: 'God, how I would hate to be an actor! Imagine Othello!'

Next he put on the old battledress blouse, the shabby one without badges, and then the small gaiters (Hilda's 'Anklets, web') and arranged the straps so that they would not flap and make a noise as he walked. (There were so many ridiculous little things that could make a deafening sound in the silent night.) Finally the cap-comforter, the short double woolly scarf which you could hollow into a cap. He pulled it on his head so that the loose end hung unevenly and shapelessly like the end of a sock. This was to give an uneven outline to the head: it helped personal camouflage. The other reason for the wool cap was that it couldn't make a sound, whereas a tin hat rattled. This had become the standard head-dress for patrols – it was warm, comfortable, and best for concealment.

As there were still a few minutes before he was due on parade, Sheldon gave himself a stiff tot of rum and settled down to smoke a final pipe, lying quite relaxed with his feet pointing towards the entrance of the dugout and his head pillowed on a haversack.

It was quiet now because it was dusk and the time of Stand To – the routine dawn and dusk manning of battle positions. It was as though the earth had stood still. He felt quite alone; and afraid.

Soon the silence was broken by the familiar thumps in the distance, followed by the flight of shells. The first lot went over high, at the height where they sound like tearing cloth; but after a couple of dozen or so of those the sound turned into a whine and whistle and they dropped quite close, over on the left and then on the right. It was only the Evening Hate – one of a methodical enemy's most regular habits – but that didn't make it less disturbing.

Now there was a scudding, sizzling whistle and sixteen came over so very low they must be for him and it was no comfort, no comfort at all, to think this was dead ground; the slope of the hill was such that their trajectory could not touch the spot, who the hell cares about trajectory, they're coming here...

The shells burst some way behind, their trajectory could not reach that dugout. Sheldon felt thick with fear. Fear. Mike Lawson. My friend Mike Lawson – late friend I should say. 'He didn't know what fear was,' some idiot wrote in the newspaper. The fool, the bloody fool, that writer. Of course he knew what fear was. Everyone knows what fear is after the first time he's afraid of the dark as a child. He knew how to overcome it, that's all. He knew how to bend fear back with the arms of will-power. He wrestled and fought with it like Laocoön with the snakes. He fooled it with feints and tricks.

(He kept his mouth shut, when others betrayed themselves by too much talk. He disconcerted it with laughter, when nothing was funny. He declined to know it socially, he constantly cut it dead. He taunted it with bravado, calculated bravado that helped him and the others.)

He fought it with love, not the love between the thighs but the sort that is in the heart of men who face perils together. So he won many rounds of this fight, old Mike. But fear grows always stronger and the muscles on the arms of will-power begin to ache, they can't bend back fear for ever. The struggle gets harder all the time. Willpower sweats and groans and aches and gasps for breath; the snakes must crush Laocoön in the end.

(The struggle was nearly over that morning he forced himself to lead them along that grass verge he knew was mined. I know this because I knew him well and I was with him before he went out that day. The mine which removed all traces that he had ever existed – well, almost all traces – was a merciful gong that merely shortened the last round.)

'He didn't know what fear was.' Do they think they honour him by saying that? Can't the idiots see that it was Prometheus walking along that grass verge, with the eagles tearing at his liver every inch of the way?

Can't they see that the whole point is not that he *didn't* know what fear was but that he *did*?

They talked about fear and courage, what does it matter anyway; that was good the other night what the Doc was saying. Some eminent medical man's definition of courage – what was it? – something about courage being moral capital and everybody having a certain amount to begin with: some more, some less, and when it has been spent it can't be replaced. That's good. That's true. Running out all the time, it is. Look through the glass panel in every man's chest and count how much is left. Young Brooks, the new subaltern, richest: he hasn't spent any yet, heap of clean new notes from England, some fivers too, lots of capital there. How much the Colonel? A few pounds yet, though how he does it I don't know, he's spent a lot, hell of a lot, must have been a millionaire to begin with – he still has a few pounds left. How about yourself, Sheldon, how much more bloody capital showing through your glass window – a few coppers?

That's about it, isn't it? A few coppers? A few bloody coppers? A few –

'Six o'clock, sir,' the voice of Perks burst in from a long way off.

'Hello, Perks, I must have dozed off.'

'It's time, sir. Is there anything I can do?' (That must be what the chaplain says when he comes to the condemned cell just before eight. But no 'sir'. At least you get a 'sir'.)

Sheldon scrambled to his feet and stepped outside.

'I'm late. Give me my stuff. Quick.'

He put on his belt, stripped except for the small compass case and a sheath-knife, he stuffed a grenade in one breast pocket, some ammunition clips in the other. 'Clean handkerchief, Perks. Quick. Handkerchief.' Then he hurried off to the patrol.

'Present and correct, sir,' murmured Sergeant Prince.

The five men stood in a single rank. With their cocoa faces and woolly scarf-caps they were a ludicrous cross between Negro minstrels and pirates, and as he walked quickly along the line inspecting them, Sheldon thought he must look even more ridiculous himself because he wore spectacles too. He walked along the rear rank checking that they had browned all exposed parts of their skin thoroughly. It sometimes happened that a man did himself up as the complete Othello, then left two large white patches behind his ears.

'Have a final check that you've nothing in your pockets that can rattle,' he ordered. 'Then issue the rum ration, Sergeant.' While the rum was being issued, he set his compass on the bearing Piecrust-White Farm: one of the bearings he had noted during the afternoon. From the foot of Piecrust, which ended the first leg of his route, the compass would come in useful.

'Right,' Sheldon said. 'You know the form. Route from here will he left foot of Piecrust, Burnt Tank Ridge, Twin Tits, Bond Street. Move from here in file: close arrowhead from Piecrust on. Oh, one other thing. The gunners are firing concentrations on White Farm for half an hour from twenty-three hundred, and they'll blast the place at midnight when we ought to be getting clear. Let's go.'

He led off at a good pace so that they could cover as much ground as possible in the half-light that would have turned into night within twenty minutes. The business of the last-minute preliminaries, the necessity to become practical and active, to give orders and to take charge, had had a tonic effect. Now that the thinking and the planning were over and the thing had started he felt a little more heartened.

The Sergeant-Major watched them disappear towards the blackening foot of Piecrust – seven Negro-minstrel pirates, identically dressed, except that one had cloth crowns on his shoulder, another stripes on his arm – and then ordered a signaller to report the patrol's departure to Battalion Headquarters.

'The White Farm patrol left at eighteen-fifteen, sir,' the Adjutant announced gravely, as though it were a special announcement for which he was interrupting the Home Service.

'Good,' the Colonel said through the six-week-old newspaper he was reading. But to himself he thought: 'No sleep tonight.' For whenever his people were doing a difficult and dangerous patrol, this old man of twenty-seven worried and fretted until they were back. He had done these patrols himself and knew what they were like: how they were a complete microcosm of battle with a beginning, middle, and end – with the added difficulty that the leader was quite on his own. He knew what they were like, the tricky ones like tonight's; and because of this, whenever one was being done, he followed them in his mind's eye all the way out and all the way back. He would sleep scarcely at all until they got back – but would force himself to keep awake, fretting and worrying: and it was this as much as anything that had turned his fair hair grey so quickly.

SEVEN

ACTION IS AN ESCAPE for the spirit. The need to concentrate thought on practical actions, however tiny, however foolish, is the most dependable of therapies. Striding through the falling night towards the left spur of Piecrust – the first stage of the long walk to White Farm – Sheldon felt better than he had felt all day. He experienced again the comfort of simplification, a comfort of which he had always been aware once an action started.

When it comes to the point war simplifies things, oversimplifies them. Get these men to that place. Go from here to there. Stay on that hill, stay on it if necessary till you are dead. War makes tiny things gigantically important for the moment.

Six adult men spend half a night and all their mental and physical energy, all their intellectual capacity, all their mental acumen and ingenuity, their skill, their endurance, their moral tenacity on the temporarily vital task of getting a small lorry containing a wanted commodity across twenty yards of thick mud. A private universe segregates a group of sappers sweating to complete a bridge before protective darkness pales into a new day and they become exposed to the accurate fury of gunners: there is nothing for them but the finishing of the bridge before dawn. The grimy private panting across country with a written message because the telephone and the wireless have failed, accepts without question that death alone must prevent his reaching his destination: even though he has no idea what is written on the dirty fragment of paper he carries or even whether it matters.

War has this one mercy of always giving you an immediate object. That's what it is. The other life is always more complex. How many men in the other life know where they are going and why? There is doubt, confusion, frustration, hesitation, bewilderment, compromise. Innumerable factors, an unclearly defined objective. At least this is so for the great majority. That is why fools and lazy men enjoy war.

This process of simplification was a great help when you were on the job. Sheldon had never been more aware of it than now, as he continued to step out on that first leg of the journey. It had been an interminable day. A day that had begun with hope when he was told that for three or four nights his company could take things more easily. Not that ordinary defensive vigilance could in any way be relaxed. But apart from the usual standing patrol and the one ambush – which were simply sentry posts pushed a little outside the Company area – there would be no other nightly commitments unless, of course, the enemy started something. No long reconnaissance and fighting patrols. It would be possible for a large proportion of the Company to sleep at night, and in those stark circumstances this brief, temporary release from extra duties seemed almost a holiday. There had been a tip, too, that the relief of the Division by another – so long promised so often postponed – might really happen quite soon: though he had been told to keep this strictly to himself so as not to raise hopes that might again have to be disappointed.

Thus had the day begun, and at last he had been given a new officer which was going to be an enormous help, a good one too, by the look of him. It truly had seemed that morning as though he could look forward to two, even three, successive nights of sleep. And then Division, damn their eyes, had ordered this patrol. Yet now that it was actually happening life was not quite so bad, because it had simplified itself. There was only one purpose now, to get to White Farm. The private universe of Tim Sheldon was a long thin strip of night, seven men wide, with White Farm at the end of it; and all he had to do for the present was to get there.

In the deepening dusk a blacker darkness upward sloping showed them they were approaching the left shoulder of Piecrust. He led them up close, to where the path fell away leftwards into a shallow ravine, and the slope of the hill rose up to the right. He stopped and the luminous dial of his wristwatch showed that they had covered this first stretch of nearly a mile in half an hour, which was good going for the night had clamped down on them fast in the last few minutes.

'From here,' he told them in a low voice, 'absolute silence. We'll go from here in arrowhead, a Bren on each flank the other Bren in the rear. Keep damn close. It's going to be hellishly dark. Not even a star. If you're likely to want a pee get it over now. Remember, absolute quiet from now on.'

While they took advantage of his suggestion, Sheldon opened his compass and aligned the luminous pointers so that it pointed along the bearing at which he had set it before leaving – the bearing that would lead from Piecrust to White Farm. He held the compass before him and tried hard to penetrate the darkness ahead, to fasten on to some prominent landmark lying in the path of the pointing compass: some mark on which he could fasten his eyes for the next stage of the march. He strained with his eyes, forcing them to pierce the blackness, but it was difficult. After a while he made out the outline of a feature, or thought he did, and keeping the compass pointing towards it he whispered to Sergeant Prince, who was at his side, to get the men quickly into formation. Then he moved off, this time moving slowly.

He led them slowly, carefully down the rocky path which curved down into the shallow ravine, and up the other side, keeping his eyes firmly on the vague shape he thought he had discerned; and as they walked along the ground which now began to slope upwards he felt reasonably certain that he was leading them accurately towards Burnt Tank Ridge, named from the tank wreck which by daylight was an invaluable landmark in an area where landmarks were scarce. He hoped that his direction was right because that is as much as any man can do in country of this kind on a black night when there are not even stars to help.

This was no man's land, eeriest of half-worlds, half-world of blackness, chilly menace, and silence except for the distant howling of dogs. Occasionally there were soft shimmerings and whines high above, indicating that the nightly artillery duels were in progress. The passage of the shells in either direction made a thin curving roof high above, but they seemed to have no connection with you or with the long thin night, seven men wide, which was your private strip of no man's land. The shells came from far ahead to far back; at this distance you seldom heard them depart or arrive; you merely knew from the faint shimmering, the occasional rustle, that they were on their way, far above you.

The ground still rose, but not steeply. Sheldon, leading them cautiously, stealthily, searched in his mind for the picture of this land he had tried so hard to print on his memory when he was studying it during the afternoon from the observation post on Piecrust. In his mind's eye he was back at the top of Piecrust, peering down at this very spot, noting its form and shape and outline. This *must* be the slope leading to Burnt Tank Ridge. The slope continued, endlessly continued, it was so hard to judge speed and distance in the dark. Probably they had covered very little distance but it seemed like miles before he was aware that no longer was it uphill. He stopped. He peered to the right and slowly across the front to the left and then back again trying to pierce the dark. Desperately he willed a portion of the darkness to resolve itself into the shape of the wrecked tank and to reassure him of his position but the darkness was adamant, and his eyes ached from the vain effort to pierce it.

To the Sergeant he whispered: 'Burnt Tank Ridge, I think'. It was neither a statement nor a question so much as a spoken thought, pleading for reassurance. The Sergeant tried to pierce the darkness, too, but he said nothing, nothing at all. It was Sheldon's job – Sheldon's alone – to get them there. As he stood there, helpless in the unyielding darkness fighting to suppress a panicky feeling that he was lost, he felt more stunningly than ever before the deep loneliness of command.

It was his job to get them there. His. His. His. He sensed the eyes of the five men watching him. The tall Sergeant at his side was a comforting presence but at this moment no more than that. He had nothing to say. No views to offer. It wasn't his job. It was Sheldon who had to decide. On an average dark night it would not have been quite so difficult, but tonight was impossible.

He must chance it. If this was the ridge he thought it was, the next point to make for was the saddle feature they called – for obvious reasons – Twin Tits. He had a bearing from Burnt Tank Ridge to

Twin Tits. Working rapidly now he fished from his pocket a shaded pencil torch and a piece of paper on which he had a list of bearings. Shading the torch with great care he flicked it on long enough to check the new bearing he now required.

'Your compass,' he whispered to the Sergeant. His own was set on the Piecrust-White Farm bearing and he didn't wish to interfere with it. Holding Sergeant Prince's compass to his eye he turned it slowly until through the pin-hole viewfinder the luminous strip of figures showed the figure he wanted. Then he moved off on the new bearing, gambling on the spot they were leaving being Burnt Tank Ridge. If it wasn't, the new bearing would be worse than useless, and they would be utterly lost. But he tried to avoid thinking of that, it was necessary to keep moving.

He continued to move slowly, for the ground was uneven, and the possibility of running into an enemy patrol or ambush was ever present. Even though this was a wide no man's land; not a tidy strip between two well organised defence lines, but an area of varying width, anything from two and a half to four miles wide. Both armies were thin on the ground, there was on neither side a close-knit defensive line, but a series of defended localities on the best bits of ground. Sometimes these were quite far from one another, for the total length of this hilly battlefront was considerable. To make up for the gaps and the lack of numbers, both armies nightly crossed this no man's land with fighting patrols and raiding parties: partly to keep tabs on the other side, partly to harass, and this mobile war within a war continued ceaselessly between the major offensives. The effect of these patrols was like that of a boxer who, by mobility and by continuous jabbing with his left, hopes to unsettle and weaken a stronger opponent.

They seemed now to be on a track, and as the surface was softer and more level than it had been, Sheldon very slightly quickened the pace, but they were still advancing at something less than a slow walk. Twice he dropped to one knee and listened intently. As he did so the rest of them dropped down too, as though they were in some way connected to his person, so instinctively did they react to his movement. Each time he thought he had heard a suspicious sound:

the first time a voice, the second footsteps, but when he listened there was nothing and none of the others could hear anything either. The only sound was that of their breathing. But the two stops had the effect of heightening the tension, increasing their alertness. On a night like this you could be within five yards or even two yards of a crouching figure before being aware of it. It was disconcerting to hear sounds of any kind. In no time at all you began to sense fingers curling round triggers, bodies wriggling into fire positions, hands raised to give a signal to fire – all of them just a foot or so away – along there – in the darkness. The fewer noises you heard or imagined that you heard the better. In a way the farm-dogs and the jackals and the shells passing high above were a comfort because there was no mistaking them. It was the faint rustle, the barely perceptible twitch, the hardly audible click that could paralyse you with fright in a split half-second as you edged your way through the uncompromising dark.

When they had been advancing in this way for some time longer, the ground to the left seemed to rise more sharply as though the track were skirting a slope. It was forty minutes since they had left Burnt Tank Ridge – if it was Burnt Tank Ridge. The mass now looming on the left could be Twin Tits. *Could* be.

He stopped, motioned the patrol to get down, and began to peer at the high ground, striving to form an impression of its outline. Perhaps the clouds had thinned out, perhaps he was becoming more used to the dark, but it was now just a little easier to see than before. He was able to pick out the outline of a feature. The only snag was that it wasn't a bit like Twin Tits. That was the trouble with these damned hills. You looked at them from some way off and they had an unmistakable shape. When you came close they were quite different. This didn't look even vaguely like Twin Tits. Hell!

He was wondering what to do next when a series flashes, from the direction whence they had come, momentarily showed up the silhouette of Piecrust. Stroke of luck! Twin Tits was in a direct line between Piecrust and White Farm. With Piecrust so conveniently picked out by gun flashes it was only a matter of seconds with a compass to establish whether this point was on that bearing or not.

He held the compass to his eye peering impatiently through the minute view-finder. As near as didn't matter it was. This must be Twin Tits.

The relief of being certain of his position was overwhelming. It was the first relaxed moment since the beginning of the patrol two hours before. A wave of tiredness suffused him. The relief from the intense concentration and anxiety of the past two hours caused him almost to collapse from fatigue. His brain was humming with reaction, and it was a minute or so before he could once again regain his power to concentrate and continue. 'This is Twin Tits,' he whispered, 'more than half way'. Then he motioned the patrol to get up.

The next stage was to the lateral road they called Bond Street. It couldn't be missed, because it ran across the front at right angles to their general line of approach. But it was important to try to hit it near the point where it joined a track which led most of the way to White Farm. He had a bearing (worked out on the map) from Twin Tits to this junction of track and road. He led off along this bearing. The ground seemed to be flattening out. It was not quite so difficult to keep more or less on a straight line. It was desperately important to find that road junction because the track practically delivered you to the doorstep of White Farm. If he could get on it it would remove from the last mile of the journey the anxieties of navigation, leaving him free to concentrate on what, after all, was the real business of the evening. In the misery of finding your way on these things you could almost forget about what was to happen when you got there. Getting there at all became the obsession, not what happened after you arrived.

With a road to aim at now, Sheldon felt slightly more relaxed, though the extreme tension of the first half of the journey had left him very tired. Sustained concentration and the aloneness of responsibility could press on the brain till you felt it must burst and you hated those with you who could not share the burden. And then, as soon as you relaxed even in a small way, fatigue rolled through the body like shock, but the gladness and relief of temporary success were a small consolation.

Now, instead of trying to identify features in the liquid velvet of transitory shapes, there was a road to find – a straight road running across your line of approach. You couldn't miss a road. So Sheldon was just that little bit more at ease as he led them, as slowly and careful as ever, towards the road they called Bond Street, a mile or so ahead. The more open ground was a mercy. The knowledge that he could not very well miss a road was a luxury. He was more confident now that he could strike it near the junction: the junction with the other road which took you to White Farm.

The measure of this partial relief from tension was that for the first time during the evening he was aware of boredom. While nine-tenths of his mind remained frozen with alertness, concentration, and the burden of leading, the other tenth slipped into boredom. The boredom of the infantryman, mute and sightless, forcing one foot past the other in rhythmical timeless progress through the night from nowhere to nowhere.

Without disturbing the nine-tenths of the mind that was set in its task like the automatic-pilot control of an aeroplane, the remaining tenth drifted into a flow of distracting consciousness, clutching at thoughts and half-thoughts that would smother if only for a few instants the ennui, the slow one-foot-after-the-other, the helpless underlying awareness of futility. Soon this became music. This was a favourite secret game of his, to play over in his mind music he knew and loved. He was not a musician but he had a profound feeling for it and an imaginative appreciation of its construction and harmonic scope so that, as he played it over in his mind, he could embroider and embellish and invent orchestrations and new variations of his own. It was a distraction he saved for the long stretches of special ennui: long rides and marches, and on patrols, when the need to move slowly added to the aching wearisome blankness. For when the night and the need for stealth make it essential to advance with this exaggerated, lingering care, every step is a deliberate tiring act. At one mile an hour the body must be held permanently in a position of strain in order that the legs may be deliberately and precisely pushed forward one after the other, and it was then that the music helped.

His other time for music was on a motor-cycle. That was particularly good because you didn't merely think the music, you could bawl out the melody and the roar of the engine drowned the noise. It was heartening to shout a melody at the top of your voice, to exult in your maximum lung-power without the embarrassment of hearing your voice. At the same time your mind could imagine the most wonderful orchestral accompaniment to the melody you were shouting but could not hear, and travelling fast along a deserted road making personal music, you could feel a tremendous exultation. Once he had done this on a downhill stretch of road, pursued by incandescent tracer shells from an anti-tank gun. Crouched low over the machine he had bawled his lungs out as the glow-balls flicked noiselessly past. That was the only one of his narrow escapes that he could remember with exhilaration, even enjoyment, and the music on that occasion had been *Petrouchka*.

The tenth of Sheldon's mind that was not leading the patrol slipped into the slow movement of Beethoven's Seventh Symphony. It was in all music the work he liked best, and he always came back to it. He knew the symphony very largely by heart, and liked all of it; but above all he loved the slow movement, loved the way it went on building, loved the way (if you were playing it over in your mind) you could march to it and keep adding to it. When you came to the end of Beethoven's variations you could invent your own in this musical omnipotence of the secret mind.

Tum tum-tum tum tum, tum tum-tum tum tum. It was perfect to march to. It was fine for ordinary marching speed and as good for the slow pace you used on patrol: you simply allowed twice the number of beats for each step, so that you could march slowly without altering the tempo of the music. You could do everything else to that slow movement of the Seventh, but you mustn't mess about with its tempo which has the gravity and inevitability of destiny. That damned Seventh is just about the best thing in music. Sheldon was thinking as he had so often thought. It is the perfect work of art, the definitive work of art. Play it in your mind for ever. Best of all the slow movement, Jesus! that slow movement. Tum tum-tum tum tum, tum tum-tum tum tum, tum tum-te tee tee...

Wonder what they're thinking, these six behind me. Perhaps nothing. The led, lucky devils, can shut off their minds. Beer and women? Not necessarily. Ten Pint Midgeley, yes. Definitely, Ten Pint would undoubtedly be thinking of beer and women. Certainly not of his peacetime job of glass-blowing – glass-blowing is fun, tried it once in Sweden, that park place near Stockholm where the national crafts are laid out on show – there's a glass place there where you can have a blow yourself. Fun. Blew much too hard. Wonder if Ten Pint is good. Wonder how many grades of glass-blowing there are and if Ten Pint is a big king in glass-blowing circles. Must go to St Helens after the war and see Ten Pint blowing. Tubbs and Tyldesley. Football and chess. Those are the things they care about, probably they think of that. Football especially. They know all the names and who was the best outside-right and all the rest of it. A study and a science, not a game. They're not good at chess but of the same level, so they have exciting games all the time. Are they thinking of cup-ties and queen's bishop? Do men like Tubbs and Tyldesley think about such things in the blankness of a patrol? It isn't necessarily beer and women. By no means. Big Bilsbury, for instance, the undertaker's assistant, knows pottery, the old stuff. Uncle in the antique business. Bilsbury worked for him once and learned. Loves china. Admitted so sheepishly once when the others couldn't hear. Perhaps he dreams of Wedgwood, Coalport, and Minton on these affairs. You never know. Men are always unexpected. Well, nearly always. Not Ginger Mobbs, the miner, though. Not beer and women for Ginger Mobbs, just women. Teetotaller. But a great one for the ladies. Strange, because what the hell is his charm? Stocky redhead, twisted nose, and, when he smiles, Gorgonzola teeth. Enough to put anyone off, but Ginger had great success. Always. No one knew why, or rather everyone assumed there could be only one reason.

There was the time at Bou Kebir, for instance, when persistent overtures had been made to the farmer's wife, overtures which the lady had repelled with some vehemence. Everyone had a go except Ginger Mobbs who waited until the very last day before the unit left: then he walked casually into the house and emerged an hour later, smiling contentedly. What was the secret, the others wanted to know? How much had it cost? Ginger smiled in a superior way. 'A tin of bully beef,' he said. A tin of bully and what else, they had wanted to know. 'Experience, my friends,' Ginger had said. 'As a matter of fact,' he had added as an afterthought, 'it were dead easy. For Spam I could 'ave 'ad 'er old man too'.

Tum tum-tum tum tum, tum tum-tum tum tum... Sergeant Prince. What about him? Dreaming of dress regulations and battalion orders? Reciting to himself the poetry of stores, pondering the philosophy of drill, soothing his senses with the aesthetics of trajectory? For these things were the world of Sergeant Prince. Tum tum-te tee tee, tum tum-te tee tee... Probably they thought of nothing, these six men. Nothing at all. It is the one privilege of those who follow to renounce thought, to bury their minds in comforting blankness, to follow blindly the one in front trusting him; and to rely on their animal instinct and developed reflexes to prick them into awareness when danger threatened. Lucky not to have to think. Why do they follow, why do they trust? Habit? A sense of job? Nice if they all deserted. Suddenly. Now. The whole lot suddenly skin off. Leave you quite alone, only yourself to worry about. You go on a bit. Wonderfully relieved of responsibility. Alone to White Farm. Clever Sheldon finished patrol all by himself. But they don't desert. While there is someone to go in front they follow: follow until body or mind gives way. And so long as they have strength to follow, the one in front must worry for them. Tum tum-tum tum tum...

He had played through the slow movement twelve or thirteen times. It was on his brain. It wouldn't go. Tum tum-tum tum tum. For ever and ever. Ran out of Beethoven's variations long ago. Own variations now, terrific variations. Four orchestras going flat out and a couple of choirs have just come in. Tremendous crescendos, and one of the choirs doing a counter-melody in triplets. High register no voice could reach. Music of the spheres, only perceptible in the upper reaches of the brain.

Sister Murgatroyd steps noiselessly into Ward Seven. Wide grey eyes behind proffered thermometer. She pats the bed, smoothing the wrinkles. Women instinctively pat any bed within reach. Sister Murgatroyd does it with great elegance. Sister Murgatroyd does everything stylishly and with elegance. She is cool, beautiful, strengthening; Mary Murgatroyd doesn't exist, never existed, there is only Sister Murgatroyd. As she pats the bed she brushes close, panting gently from her exertions. Nice exertions. The gasps are just perceptible and close, there is for an instant the gentlest waft of cool clean breath close to your brow. Tum tum-tum tum tum. This slow movement of the Seventh is the sublimest of sublime. I would like to die copulating to it. Do you ever think of music you would like to die copulating to? Debussy, perhaps? No, not big enough. The Liebestod? No, too obvious much too obvious. This slow movement is the one. Sublime noise, sublimest noise. Please, God, please, Sister Murgatroyd, I want to die copulating to the slow movement of the Seventh. Tum tum-tum tum tum, tum tum-tum tum tum...

A pressure on the shoulder. Sheldon dropped quickly to one knee, and the others did the same. They subsided noiselessly, as one. The Sergeant, who had pressed on Sheldon's shoulder, pointed ahead. He peered and his eyes made out a faint line that was greyer than the rest of the night. Bond Street was a few yards ahead. He signalled them forward until they were just short of the edge of the road, then he motioned them down again. They went down quickly, still in formation, grateful for a rest. Sheldon noted that it was nearly twenty-one-thirty.

He reckoned that they had covered about three and a half miles in the three hours and a quarter they had been out. If he could find the track running out of Bond Street at right angles, they would be within a mile or so of their objective. An easy mile if he could only find the track. That now was the problem, to find that track.

They were well into the middle of the plain, and Bond Street was a goodish secondary road which cut across its middle. Like most of the roads in this country it was bordered by nothing except the shallowest of ditches. The point was which way to look first for the track. It was a toss-up whether to go right or left up Bond Street. If only another of those gun flashes would light up Piecrust, he could get a bearing and judge from that. But he had had his ration of luck for the journey. Though numerous faint gun flashes constantly flickered to their rear, none lit up Piecrust, the only landmark that would have been unmistakable. Left or right? Oh, dear. He must decide quickly. No use keeping them hanging about uncertainly. Left or right? He decided to go to the right. There was no reason for his choice; he made it instinctively. Something had to be decided. But before setting off he took the precaution of ordering the patrol to wait, then, alone, he went a short distance up the road leftwards, just to make certain that the track wasn't a few yards away in that direction. When he had established this, he returned to the patrol and led them off to the right, following the line of the road but keeping just off it. With the road as guide it was possible to move rather quickly.

They covered some five hundred yards, and there was no sign of the track. The old fear of being lost began to grip him. Perhaps this wasn't Bond Street. Perhaps when he went left by himself he had not gone far enough, perhaps the track was only a few yards beyond the point at which he had turned back. Was it worth just going on like this? Or should he turn off and try to make it across country? Another hundred yards, try another hundred. No junction. Another fifty. No junction. He was close to panic. He stared desperately into the dark trying to force his eyes to see, so that they ached more than ever, and he noticed that he was sweating: the sweat was dripping from his eyebrows on to his glasses, so that he had to wipe them. He sensed that the eyes of men were drilling into the back of his neck, so that it felt prickly. Being lost when you are the leader is the worst thing of all. He hated them because he was lost, and could feel their eyes behind him. He hated them because the whole patrol was unnecessary and silly, and because on a night like this it was utterly impossible to find your way. Rage and despair were welling up inside him so that he thought he must let out a great cry, when his foot crunched and he saw that he had stepped on to the gritty hardness of a track. He loved them then and wanted to cry, but for joy.

While the patrol lay prone, their weapons thrust automatically into fire positions, Sheldon closely examined the junction. It was a T-junction, all right. The track was a clearly defined one, even in the dark. By the standards of the country almost a third-class road. The map showed only one T-junction on this sector of the road. This should be it. He had one way of checking. Studying the ground during his reconnaissance from Piecrust, he had noticed a thick clump of cactus a short distance from the junction. He ordered the Sergeant to take a Sten gunner and see if he could find it.

Soon after they had gone he began to fret and wish that he had gone himself. Why were they taking so long? They were taking an age. They were probably looking for the cactus in the wrong place. Damn. Why didn't he go himself! They should have been back by now. Where the hell had they got to?

But he could have embraced the Sergeant when he appeared out of the night and whispered that he had found the cactus. It didn't matter that he had been away for hours because he had found it. (Actually, the Sergeant had been absent for less than ten minutes.)

Having signalled the men to huddle in close, Sheldon whispered to them that this was the last stretch. About a mile. They would advance along the line of the track but keeping to the right of it.

Tum tum-tum tum tum, tum tum-tum tum tum. The nine-tenths of Sheldon's mind, the automatic pilot, led them along the right of the track, and the other tenth returned to the slow movement of the Seventh with new strength. With the track to guide them, the only problem now was silence and alertness. Anywhere now they might run into trouble. An outpost. An ambush. A working party setting mines or putting up wire. A patrol from the other side. He placed his feet, one before the other, with the care of a young woman practising deportment. When the ground was hard he placed the ball of the foot down first, when it was soft the heel. This was the way to achieve absolute silence, and he achieved it. He walked as though he had books balanced on his head, the men close to him in arrowhead formation, and by his example and his tenseness he willed them into as disciplined a motion as himself. He had a little more than an hour in which to reach the lying-up position near White Farm. At twenty-three-hundred the Artillery were to fire concentrations on the place until twenty-three-thirty. The purpose was partly to harass the target, but mainly to act as a guide to the patrol. The shells, arriving on a target accurately registered in advance, would help the patrol to identify it. For on a night like this you could be right on top of a building before you were aware of it. Tum tum-tum tum tum...

Sheldon subsided rapidly and with him the others. His heart froze till it hurt. Unmistakably the sound of footsteps somewhere to the right and coming nearer. The seven men pressed themselves into the hard ground, heedless of the sharp stones which cut into their flesh and bruised their bones: there was silence except for the gale of their breathing and the thunder of heartbeats, as the crunch of the boots came nearer. Sheldon knew that he was sweating because his glasses were again steamed up – even in the dark he could tell; then the sweat again dripped from his eyebrows, dripping down the lenses of his glasses and onto his face so that he tasted salt. He took off the glasses, not breathing while he did so, and wiped them, and the crunch of the boots became no louder and then began to fade till finally it faded into nothing. Boche patrol? Arab walking in boots taken from a soldier's grave?

They lay there until Sheldon could make the effort to shake out of his paralysis and get up. He got them moving again, but his mind no longer played the slow movement. It needed the whole of his will now to go on, to keep placing one foot after the other, so delicately, like a girl learning to walk correctly. With books on her head. And when they had walked with books on their heads for another period of timelessness they came to the place where the track forked into three directions, and he knew that they had arrived.

They were within four hundred yards of White Farm – somewhere in the blackness forward and to their left. It was nine minutes to twenty-three-hundred when the shells of the Artillery were to start pin-pointing the farm with their explosions. He had nine minutes in which to find a place with cover where they would lie up and watch the supporting gunfire and find a position to use as a start-point for the final approach to the farm itself – if it were possible to get any nearer to it.

He headed up the leftmost of the three forks and hoped he might find a ditch or a wall. The ground, however, was still open though it undulated slightly, and when he came to a small mound, which appeared to be hollowed out to some extent like a bunker on a golf-course, he decided that that was the best he was likely to find for the moment. Having seen that the patrol had taken up the best protective fire positions possible in the circumstances, he settled down to wait for the guns which would be opening up in four minutes, and would be their final signpost.

His immediate feeling was one of indescribable relief at having got there. He was utterly tired after the nightmare journey. It was as if to get there had been the sole object of the operation. They would never know what he had gone through. No one would care about the journey. No one would think twice about his having found his way through the long night in country like this, in darkness of this viscous intensity. He felt limp with gladness and injustice and self-pity, one emotion quickly giving way to another. Again his spectacles were steamed up, and all of a sudden the blister on his right foot began to tingle. He had been unaware of it on the march, but now that the tension was eased, he felt the blister even though he was not standing on it. It might be bad on the way back.

Punctually at twenty-three-hundred the first shells came over. The guns were too far back to be audible. There was simply a lazy sighing followed by a series of echoing crashes forward and to the left. Then more: and more: then silence. Sheldon and the men strained with their eyes in the direction of the explosions, trying to see as well as hear them. When, after a short interval, further salvoes came over, it was just possible to discern faint flashes. But these shells made very little flash and it was difficult to spot them. But he saw enough to be certain exactly where the farm was. He estimated that he must be within three hundred yards. The shells were encouraging not because they might be hurting someone – they seemed strangely mild in their casual intermittence and their by no means thunderous effect – but because they meant that now he was not entirely alone. Someone back there was with him. It was nearly five hours since they had set out. He had been through five hours of continuous strain and anxiety and fear, and he had had to bear it alone. The arrival of these shells on time and on the right spot gave him a small reassurance that he wasn't entirely forgotten.

(But why did one's own shells always seem less fearful than the other people's? They sounded such polite shells. So tidy in the noise of their burst.)

The sighing continued in intermittent salvoes. For it was part of the plan that the shelling should not be purposeful enough to arouse enemy suspicions that something special was brewing. Then one of the shells hit something inflammable. There was a momentary flare-up and for an instant the front of a white house lit up and Sheldon saw that it was little more than the three hundred yards distance that he had estimated. In the same split second he saw a bank fifty yards ahead of where they were and decided that it would be a better position in which to lie up. It was not much nearer to the house, but more to a flank, and it was near other cover which would be useful when the time came to withdraw.

He had seen no sign of movement during the brief lighting up of the farm. He began to feel that perhaps there was a chance that Division were right. Perhaps the place really was unoccupied now. He was about to lead the patrol forward to the next position when his heart, tired by many spasms of fear that night, was struck by yet another. A shell had again caused a momentary flare-up, and in its light he had distinctly seen a figure walk out of the house and hurry into the shadows on the left. For a time he could not move. The expected can happen with a shock of unexpectedness. The wish, perhaps, had fathered the subconscious thought that the farm would be empty, that the anticipatory fear would in the end prove to have been unnecessary. In the dramatic appearance of a single human being the worst fears were now finally confirmed.

He knew he must move now or he never would. He made a supreme effort and led the way to the bank, crawling. They crawled, using their elbows as paws, so that their hands could hold their weapons at the ready, and they worked their legs in great heaves from the instep so that it was as though they were swimming on land. They wriggled and squirmed and heaved their way over the harsh cutting ground, scarcely aware of the cuts they were receiving, so great was the fear driving them across the fifty yards to the bank: the precious desirable bank that was to be their safer next position, and it was just as they had reached it and wriggled into fire positions and began to feel their newest cuts and bruises that the night exploded.

From eight points machine guns opened fire and the streams of red tracer tore through the dark along neatly interlocking lines of fire: the fixed lines on which guns are defensively set at night, and then more guns started up from the distant flank. The light mortar bombs began to explode to the left, and farther back the heavy mortars, with dull thuds.

Only the Artillery SOS to come, Sheldon thought. He knew this pattern of night defensive fire by heart. The night fire plan is the same in any language; he had so often devised this kind of plan himself. No sooner had he had the thought than the shells began screaming down on the SOS target – the point where the defenders of any position consider they are most likely to trap the attackers as they form up for their final assault. At night you cannot aim your guns, so you must place them in advance where you think they may do the most good if you are attacked by an enemy you cannot see. This was the firing which continued now with maximum ferocity for five dreadful minutes, but mostly it was to the left and rear of where the patrol cowered against their protective bank. It seemed that Sheldon had chosen the approach from which the enemy least expected attack. The guns stopped as suddenly as they had begun. They had been firing for five minutes.

They must have spotted us, all right, Sheldon thought. Then lost us. They've finished blazing away on their fixed lines. We can get away now. We've got the information we were sent to get. White Farm is quite deserted except for about a battalion. Please inform Divisional Intelligence with my compliments. There was no point in staying any longer. They had their information. They had provoked a full-scale firework display. They had managed not to get hit. He was debating whether to get out immediately or lie low a little longer when he had another shock.

Five men were approaching in extended order. Again the unexpectedness of the expected: they were suddenly close, because it would not have been possible to see them until they were near. He had only time to pray that none of his men would lose his nerve and fire too soon. Now the fat was going to be in the fire. The five Germans were advancing straight at them. They had obviously been sent out to search for him. He daren't issue an order – he would have been heard. He could only grip his Sten tightly and hope that his men would control their trigger fingers and wait. He held his breath until the approaching section was five yards away, four yards... then he gave the order for rapid fire. Three Brens and three Stens poured into them and only one of the five died slowly enough to let out a single scream for his mother as he did so. The centre man, an officer, fell forward on to the bank just to the right of Sheldon.

Sheldon pulled out his sheath-knife and quickly hacked at the collar of the dead officer, cutting off the part bearing the number of his unit, and as he stuffed it into his pocket he ordered the withdrawal. At once the patrol swept into the automatic routine they had practised so many times but had never yet used in action. And the enemy opened fire again, and blazed away with even greater intensity along their fixed lines, as they had done before, but now there were still more guns brought into action including some far over on the left.

Without hesitation Sheldon's patrol began their automatic withdrawal. The leading two Brens at once began to blaze away and under their cover the rest of the patrol sprinted back about fifty yards, where the third Bren started firing. As soon as the third Bren opened fire, the forward two doubled back to a position behind the rest of the patrol and again began to fire. As soon as they had started to do so the third Bren – the one now out in front – withdrew to a position still further to the rear of the patrol.

This leap-frogging of the Brens continued in short bounds so that there was always covering fire for the group moving back, and the proportion of tracer in their ammunition gave them a direction guide and also ensured that they did not run into their own fire. But this same tracer had the disadvantage of giving away their position, and though they were changing their fire positions rapidly and had soon got some way clear of the farm area, the enemy mortars began to seek them out. The enemy fixed lines were blazing away without pause, but Sheldon had withdrawn back and to the right and now he had the advantage of a number of out-buildings and walled yards which shielded the patrol from view whenever a flare lit up the night. By the light of one of them Sheldon saw a portion of broken wall some distance to his rear, and as soon as the flare had died away he led the patrol in a swift dash back to it, this without covering fire that would betray the line of their withdrawal: it was a piece of rapid thinking which prompted him to this interruption of the automatic plan; and, by breaking the continuity of his fire, to complete a further stage of the withdrawal without giving away his direction. They reached the wall, and took up position behind it, gasping with pain and fear and exhaustion. They crouched for a time behind its cover, and the enemy fire began to quiet down except for a couple of persistent mortars which were scattering their fire haphazard about the front, hoping for the best, and some of their bombs were falling uncomfortably close. Then shells began to pass over from behind, and Sheldon realised that it must be midnight. That was the pre-arranged time at which their own Artillery were to give White Farm a final fifteen-minute pounding. This was intended to coincide with the time at which the patrol was likely to be pulling out. It wasn't harassing fire this time but a thorough dosing, and it heartened them a little to hear the shells crashing about the farm. It was heartening, too, that they seemed quite a distance away, an indication of the yards the patrol had covered in their swift but controlled dashes.

Now was the time to get moving again, while the gunners were keeping the farm occupied. If only those enemy mortars would stop. Sheldon had just decided to risk making a dash for it when a couple of bombs fell quite close and a third landed between Tubbs and Tyldesley. Tubbs died without a sound and Tyldesley wasn't scratched. Sergeant Prince, the professional, knelt swiftly and removed from the dead man's pockets the ammunition he would no longer need, and distributed it among the others.

'We've got to get back across Bond Street as quick as we can,' Sheldon whispered. Once they were safely across the road, the plain soon broke up into undulating ground through which they could reach the safety of the hills. Bond Street was in a sense a finishing post. The new immediate objective. All we've got to do is to skin across this plain, he thought, and hurry to the other side of Bond Street.

The darkness that had nearly broken his spirit was now his greatest comfort: caressing, protective, lovely dark. The tracks no longer mattered. The only thing now was to get across to the hills beyond the road called Bond Street. He took a rough bearing and led the surviving quintet rapidly across the hard flat ground, at a pace somewhere between a fast walk and a stumbling run. Often they tripped on the sharp, flinty stones, and once one of the Brens was dropped, but now speed was the most important thing, not silence. They had to get to the road, and they must chance running into any enemy patrols that might by ill-luck be about. The mortars continued to follow them, scattering their bombs about the night, sometimes they came close, sometimes they were far away. They were still searching and hoping for the best. It was as though the long arms of a pair of phenomenal derricks were reaching high into the night sky, and swaying from side to side, to drop the small but vicious bombs on the men who were making a dash for safety.

They were well on their way towards the road when the gentle shush of mortar bombs sounded directly above. They flung themselves down, and seven bombs fell around them with sickening crashes, and then after an interval an eighth, and it was after that one that Sheldon felt a shearing pain in his left leg. He gave a grunting cry and the Sergeant was instantly at his side.

'Where did it get you, sir?'

'Leg.'

The sergeant gently felt the joints and helped him to his feet.

'I'm all right. Got to keep moving. We've got to get to the road.'

As if they knew of their success the mortars gave up, and soon the shelling of the farm stopped. That meant it was a quarter-past midnight: just six hours since the patrol had set out. Sheldon felt the warm blood trickling down his leg. As it had trickled down the other leg when he was wounded before, but there seemed more of it this time. Before, it had been a bullet: this time it was shrapnel. A bigger gash. The blood trickled down into his boot and the leg began to feel heavier, but he dragged it along – he must keep going. Then the blister on the other foot began to twinge, and that struck him as funny. When the Sergeant tried to help him he brushed him aside.

'I'm all right,' Sheldon said, almost sourly. 'I'm all right. We've got to keep going. We've got to get beyond that road.'

They walked and stumbled and panted, six where there had been seven, shuffling and stumbling in extended line, not too extended because of getting separated in the dark, but far enough apart for the same bomb or shell, if more came, not to get two of them. No longer did they bother about the sound of their feet, speed was what mattered. And to get to the road and across it into the mounds and bumps and hills that had made the outward journey hell but would now be their protection from pursuit. When, after some fifteen minutes, they stepped across this road it was as though they were stepping into ultimate tranquillity, so transient and relative are the circumstantial climaxes of combat.

He led them on towards the hills, and very soon the ground began to rise and they came to a pimple which they skirted. Behind it there was a hollow, and Sheldon led them swiftly down into it and they flopped to the ground. For some moments they were quite still, there was only the sound of their panting and gasping, and also the falsetto of Ten Pint Midgeley whose adenoids were bad. Bilsbury the undertaker's assistant was instantly asleep and the Sergeant had to shake him and remind him that they were not yet home.

'Must get a dressing on that leg, sir,' the Sergeant said.

Sheldon pulled out his own field dressing, but the Sergeant had already opened his own. Carefully he pulled down Sheldon's trousers. The leg was a congealing mass of blood. The wound was in the thigh about four inches above the knee and on the outside of the leg. It was about two inches long and had luckily missed the bone. But it was painful. The night air blew coldly about his bare legs and privates and Sheldon began to shiver as the Sergeant wound the bandage round the gash.

'Those bloody medicos would have cut the trouser leg off,' he said, forcing a smile which became a wince as the bandage pressed a wave of pain through the thigh.

'Yes' – he spoke jerkily through thumps of pain – 'I had to spend four weeks with only one trouser leg the last time. I couldn't – easy Sergeant – go into Algiers. Because – that's better – I'd only one damn trouser leg.'

The four men watched the bandaging. They were still breathing heavily. They did not speak. They were still recovering from the tautness of fear and exhaustion. They were only just out of a mental freeze and would take time to melt. No one mentioned Tubbs: they knew how Tyldesley would be feeling.

'That's a lot better,' Sheldon said, pulling his trousers up. 'Thank you, Sergeant.'

EIGHT

HE HAD GOT THEM to the place. He had got them out, together with the information which was the object of the mission. Now he must get them back. The inexorable pattern had still to be completed. First the interminable Getting There. Then the There – the brief wild nightmare, the confused terror of the tiny night battle. Now the Getting Back: for the job would not be done until he had taken these men and that information safely back.

He wanted to rest a little longer, but he knew that it would be dangerous. Very soon now a reaction would overwhelm them and they would sink into a deep sleep, and it would be impossible to set them moving again. He knew that in such circumstances men can be so submerged in sleep that they cannot be awakened even though you kick and shake them savagely. It was important to move at once. He twisted awkwardly but quickly to his feet so that he was standing before their dulled senses could stir them to help him.

'We must get going,' he said, 'or we shall be late for breakfast.' The Sergeant followed up the order in an imperative whisper. 'On your feet, now. Hurry up. The sooner we're off the sooner we're there. On your feet.' As they shuffled into position he turned to Sheldon:

'Can I give you an arm, sir?'

'No, thanks. I'm all right.'

'Sure, sir? Let me help you.'

'I'm all right,' Sheldon breathed testily.

They moved away in file, two ranks of three with Sheldon at the head of one, Sergeant Prince at the head of the other. The leg was hurting, but the tight bandage had stopped the bleeding and in addition it was bracing the knee-joint. He would manage. He wasn't so worried about direction now. He would trust to instinct to keep them going on their present line. The right direction was due west. As soon as the first glimmering of dawn appeared about five he would simply aim away from it. If he'd gone astray he could correct direction then. The important thing now was to get those worn-out legs and bodies moving and keep them moving. They were still well on the wrong side of no man's land, with a hard three and half miles to cover; there was no time to lose. The wounded leg felt leaden and thick. Each time he stepped on it his weight sent through it a gust of pain, but he kept telling himself that so long as he kept going it would not become worse. Only if he stopped would it stiffen. Like a swimmer he had to keep going, keep going, past the point of wanting to stop. Then it would settle into a rhythm, the infantry rhythm, the automatous left right, left right, keep moving, left right...

Had it been the worst ever? It was always the worst ever. *Courage is moral capital*. How much left in the bank now? Six overdrafts here, Doc! And no security. How nonsensical these little battles were when you looked back on them. Was it all for *that*? How good the men had been. Any but the best would have lost their nerve and blazed away when they saw that line of men so close in front. But they waited for an order and so we bagged the lot. If one man had loosed off too soon it would have been we who would have been destroyed or put in the bag. It isn't shooting that's hard but *not* shooting. You must have the best men for these jobs. One weak one and everyone else pays the penalty. In a large battle it doesn't matter so much, the good ones carry the bad; Christ, I was frightened. I still am, though now there is nothing to be afraid of – not even getting lost, because you can't lose yourself once the dawn starts and all you have to do is walk away from it. In films people walk *into* the dawn, don't they? Funny! Nothing to be afraid of anymore, but still frightened. Does fear produce a hang-over? Oh, God! This leg aches. They've got a hang-over too, these other five. You can tell. They're still afraid from earlier on. Fear. Always it comes back to that. Men do strange things to overcome it. The Colonel hates shelling, loathes shelling. He admits it. So what did he do that time they pasted the command post so hard? He said, 'Nothing is going to interfere with my morning constitutional,' and walked deliberately out of the building and across to the latrine where there was no protection except a strip of canvas. He didn't have to do that, didn't have to sit there for ten minutes pretending to read a newspaper.

And poor old Simpson, a barrister, acid and cynical when he first came to us. All of a sudden he takes to reading the Bible like mad before actions. You'd find him in corners reading it feverishly, greedily. He hadn't changed inside as far as you could see. Get him somewhere quiet with a glass of something in his hand and all the smooth self-assurance of the Middle Temple gleamed as usual. But before an operation he pored over that Bible as if it were a totem. Cannon's mouth Christianity. Poor Simpson, it made no difference. S-mines do not recognise God...

Keep going, left right, keep going, left right, God Almighty! this leg hurts: hope I don't pass out...

Sergeant Prince is fine to have about. He seems miles away but every time I stumble a long arm is under my shoulders before I am aware that he has even moved. You must hand it to the regular – the best of them, anyway. They have something we can never acquire. Soldiering at its highest level is being not doing. A conditioning of the spirit and personality from childhood. We can learn to do the job for a time but we can't be that thing. Colonel Jimmie. At twenty-seven he holds a shattered, under-strength battalion together. I couldn't do that. I do a job. He is a certain kind of person.

They have something, the regulars. Not, of course, the boneheads who fetch up running reinforcements; or harmlessly in charge of army schools which others run. Not the cosy majors who potter about regimental depots teaching new officers table manners. Not the fourth-raters who use a staff captain's armlet as an excuse for waspish display of minor power. Not those, but the ones who emerge in war: when no one minds your being too young as it's only dying you've got to do, and they can always pull you down in rank afterwards. But, Jesus! they can drive you mad sometimes, those regulars: with their mixture of conservatism and gullibility. If the Brigadier says the comedy is funny then funny it is, don't dare say you thought it terrible. No such thing as not caring to hunt: hunting is correct – you must hunt. And their wives! Those parched numbers from India who love rank more dearly than their husbands. Yet so receptive (these same diehards) to anyone officially classified as an expert. They adore experts. The new craze for psychiatry, for instance. 'Trick Cyclists' they were to begin with: till the High Command took them up in a big way. Now it's the thing. 'This psychiatry business, old boy... the General's very keen on it.' Uncritically accepting something outside their ken they litter the back areas with psychiatrists and are pained because the bad soldier takes advantage of them. But still the best of those regulars have something we can never know. Like Colonel Jimmie and Sergeant Prince.

Soon it will be light. Soon it must be light. Wish the leg wouldn't throb with every step. And that damn blister's hurting again. Hope to hell I don't pass out. Must keep going. Keep going. Keep going.

Feeling in his pocket for his handkerchief, Sheldon felt the patch of cloth he had ripped off the shoulder of the German officer. He had forgotten all about it. It pleased him to think that he had remembered about the identification. It added the finishing touch to a patrol to get something like that. He felt very pleased with himself. In that climactic moment of terror and chaos he had remembered and had risked a vital second's delay in starting the withdrawal, to do the correct thing. It was more than that. It was the final irrefutable evidence that what he would be reporting was true. Not that he would have to fight to be believed. But it placed beyond all doubt the claim that you had been where you said, done what you said. That you had had a battle. That you knew what you were talking about.

At the Battalion it didn't matter. They would accept without question what you said. But those clever Intelligence boys, the experts with their Big Picture, their omniscience, and their psychic access to the enemy mind – they, damn them, were fully capable of saying: 'Obviously the fool went to the wrong place!' It was for them that you needed that precious shoulder patch whose colour and numeral revealed infallibly to which unit of which formation the owner belonged. It was for them that you wanted that silly bit of cloth. For the ones who had caused you to be sent to that place tonight because they were certain the enemy were not there.

It was the last refinement of spitting in the face of the great Intelligence myth, the Big Picture, and all the rest of it.

It was well after four now, and soon it would be first-light. The effort of forcing one leg past the other was wholly absorbing. He could hardly think of anything except the next step. How many steps more? Like a child crossing off the days of a school term he wanted to cross off a step each time he made one and watch the total grow less. Mustn't give up now. Nearly home. Left right. Nearly home. Left right.

The tiny arc of grey; the unmistakable slivering; the night is not quite so dark. It was over there. The first shy tentative incipience of a new day, as yet so faint. But six pairs of tortured eyes looked back to it in worshipful obeisance, and through their aching watched for it to grow. Nobody spoke. They all knew.

To a returning patrol first light is sacred and miraculous: not the dawning of a new day but of a new life. In the growing light the terrors of the night dissolve. The monstrous mountains contract till they are only small mounds and pimples after all. The uneven ocean through which the route has passed is a gentle valley along which winds a good path, now that you can see it. Black and evil shapes have simply vanished. The blackness, pregnant with ambush and menace, through which you have tiptoed for many hours, fades. You can smoke, you can talk: the precious way home is clear and quick.

The first grey glimmer over the enemy lines whence they had come was enough for Sheldon to see that he hadn't aimed badly though he had gone too far to the left. Within a few minutes it was light enough to make out Piecrust; there was orange mixing with the grey; the patrol were quickening their pace in new hope. It was a quarter-past five. They had been out eleven hours.

Even with the pain of his leg Sheldon was able to quicken the pace. A mile and a half to go, perhaps a little more: he had taken them quite a bit to the left. But wondrous daylight, marvellous daylight! Now they were as good as home. He glanced back at them, and he saw that they were smiling.

With daylight Sheldon realised for the first time that he would be going back. Once again he was a *pauvre blessé*. How strange! Till then it had not occurred to him that he was going anywhere but to the Battalion. To get them back there had been his single-minded intention ever since he had been hit. The Battalion would be the end of all trouble, all pain. The Battalion was the end of the road. Not once on the long march had it occurred to him that once again he had earned the rest of the *pauvre blessé*; the ambulances, the tea, the hospital train, the hospital, Sister Murgatroyd, Sister Murgatroyd!

In a day or two he would be back, perhaps in the same bed, and Sister Murgatroyd would be there to fuss over him and look after him. This time it wouldn't take so long. They were more organised than they were when he was last wounded. No more tents and male orderlies. They were even flying some of the wounded back now. For all he knew he might be in Algiers tomorrow. Wonderful thought. The leg was aching, aching mercilessly. Occasionally there was for no apparent reason a darting pain through its whole length. But now he could bear it better because there was nothing else to think of. Getting back was no longer a problem. The mind and the brain were at last set free from the night's tyranny. No more thinking, worrying, direction-finding, listening, feeling, sensing. It was the last stage of an easy walk home. The tired mind smiled, relishing its freedom.

To the Battalion briefly, and then to Algiers. How strange not to have thought of it before. Could have gloated in anticipation all night but it never occurred to me. All night could have gloated over the thought of a delicious long rest, the clean hospital, the long, long sleep, the petting, fussing, scolding nurse. No more danger; no more fear; the job was done; home soon. He limped with new heart, calling on the last reserve of his strength. He dragged the tormenting leg with a power that was compounded of relief and defiance. The travail was nearly over. Soon they would be back. Nothing to fear now. Nothing.

Sergeant Prince saw them first. He shouted, and the experienced reflexes responded on the instant and in no time they had thrown themselves to the ground. Ahead, flying low over a crest, two slit-eyes, evilly winking against the morning sky, rushed soundlessly towards them, the roar of their engines following some way behind. Jesus! Not this too!

They had spread themselves, and now they lay pressing the ground. Sheldon even pressed his wounded leg downward on the hard earth, so instinctive is this vain action even when it doubles existing pain. The white-hot glow-balls spurted from the Messerschmitt's cannon with the glib of profuseness of Roman candles, with the lightness of fairground ping-pong balls cascading joyously on jets of water. It was as delicate as that until they bit the ground, tracing along it four neat lines of small explosions, black and vicious, two from each aircraft: and with the cannon shells they sprayed machine gun bullets. In a few seconds the planes had shuddered and rasped a few feet overhead. Turning his head, Sheldon saw that no one was hit. The petrifying effect of the attack was such that it was some time before he could trust his voice to shout to them to keep down until it was certain that the machines were not returning. Before he had broken the spell in which he was held, they were on their way back to renew the attack. They were sweeping round in a wide arc. Then they dipped behind a hill and the next thing they were coming in once more from directly in front. If the sky had been clear of cloud they would have been invisible in the morning sun.

Again the white-hot glow-balls, the shower of bullets, the shuddering flight so low overhead; and one of the glow-balls flogged the back of Tyldesley, jerking on his back where he lay quite still, staring upward with eyes whose white was grotesquely exaggerated by the face, cocoa-coloured for the patrol. The woolly cap – the cap they were all wearing – added a final touch of obscene fantasy. Othello, in a pirate cap, rolling his eyes in melodramatic death.

Sheldon struggled to his feet. His leg was now on fire from the additional bruising it had just received when he flung himself down, but he made himself rise before the others. He walked over to where Tyldesley lay. He took the woolly cap off his head and shook it back into a scarf. He closed the staring eyes and covered the face with the scarf.

'We'll send a stretcher party for him. Let's go.' Tubbs and Tyldesley had died, as they had met, in alphabetical order.

So they set off once again, urging the nearly spent limbs yet again into motion, pushing towards the crest, less than half a mile ahead, beyond which lay the Battalion – the Battalion that was home. Sheldon's leg was now in such agony that when Sergeant Prince placed an arm under his shoulders and Ten Pint Midgeley unobtrusively slipped forward to support him on the other side, he did not resist.

I am going home, going home. Going home to darling Sister Murgatroyd. I'm coming back to you – pat the bed and lean close, close, so I feel the cool breath, so I look deep in the wide grey eyes, lovely eyes – let me feel the cool starch of the apron, cool me with the starch – I want everything cool because it is burning hot – I am on fire – hold the lips close so I can want and want and get better quick, then we go out and kiss the lips – want to kiss the lips always, I am hurt – I need you, darling, need you, hurt so bad – when a man is hurt he needs woman, all women, you are all women, darling Sister...

'Nearly there, sir.' The voice of Sergeant Prince from a long way off, getting louder.

'Christ!' Sheldon said. 'I must have passed out.'

'I think you just fell asleep on your feet, sir,' the Sergeant said. He and Midgeley were still supporting him.

'I've often known it happen. In India I've known men march for miles, out on their feet. Right out.'

'What was I talking about?'

'You didn't speak, sir. You were just asleep. Marching same as we are now. Not much farther.'

They came to the crest and below were the Company lines, and the Sergeant-Major saw them and ran to the telephone to report to Battalion Headquarters that they were back.

'Thanks,' Sheldon said, 'I feel fine now. I can manage. Thanks.' He shook himself free of them so that he could lead the patrol into the Company lines, subconsciously stiffening the spent body, punishing the aching leg into movement. It was six-fifteen. They had been out for twelve hours.

He led them straight to where the field cooker was snarling, and halted them close by.

'That's that,' he said. 'I expect you're ready for some breakfast. Unload the weapons and inspect them, Sergeant Prince.'

While the Sergeant did this Sheldon went up to the cook and – though it wasn't necessary – told him the patrol were to have as much extra breakfast as could be spared. When he saw that each man had a mug of tea he accepted one himself and drank it with them.

He told them they had done well. He chatted with Ainsworth and Brooks and others of the company who were about, and Perks, his batman, brought him water and a towel so that he could wash the cocoa and the dirt and sweat off his face. The men of the patrol ate their breakfast in silence, not one of them spoke, nor did they smile.

The officers tried to persuade him to let the Company stretcher-bearers carry him to Battalion Headquarters, but freshened by the wash and the tea he refused. The batman produced a stick and Sheldon set off for Battalion, the batman walking with him.

'What does he want to walk for? Why doesn't he let them carry him down?'

'He says he's all right.'

NINE

HE LIMPED STEADILY down the hill towards Battalion Headquarters, using the stick as a support. But whenever the batman tried to help him he refused, once quite sharply, as though he were engaged on something which he had to finish alone. So Perks loped sadly at his side like a dog, wanting to help but not knowing how. They didn't talk. When Battalion was still some way off they saw the Colonel approaching to meet them.

'Hello, Tim, how do you feel? You oughtn't to be walking, why didn't you come on a stretcher?'

'I'm fine, sir. It's not too bad. Only the leg again.'

'It's getting to be a habit,' the Colonel said.

'Yes. Other leg, though, this time. One mustn't repeat oneself. You heard I had two men killed?'

'Yes. Bad, that. Are you sure you're all right walking, Tim?'

'Yes, thanks,' Sheldon said. 'Just a little tired, that's all. It was a long walk.'

'Tell me about it. Unless you'd rather wait till we get down there and you can lie down.'

'No, sir. I'm all right. There isn't much to tell. We got out there a bit before eleven. Managed to get well inside the area close to the house...'

When they arrived at the dugout used as Regimental Aid Post, the Colonel saw Sheldon inside and onto a stretcher. Then he went to his own dugout to telephone a preliminary report on the patrol to Brigade.

In a daze of sweet sickness Sheldon watched the Doctor and his assistants go swiftly to work, only semi-consciously aware that his was the body which they were tending.

So wonderful to relax. His trouser leg was quickly cut off, a mug of tea found his hand, a cigarette his mouth. The ascetic face of the doctor bent low, and he dabbed at the dirty wound, with cleansing, cooling antiseptic. So wonderful to give in to it; so weary, nothing matters, I like everybody. The Doc is wonderful. Deftly, efficiently, he cleans the wound, hurts and cleans, hurts and cleans, good man, the Doc. The medical sergeant is good too. And the stretcher-bearers. Hadn't noticed they were so small: strong khaki dwarfs dispensing tea and cigarettes, endless tea, delicious sweet tea from a dark corner of the little earth room, the Regimental Aid Post, hole in a bank along a gully, the best hospital in the world – that hurt, that hurt a lot, Doc – the gentleness of rough men, bearded dwarf-nurses in battledress – the romantic glamour of the red cross, a pretty symbol – I will sleep for ever – what's that? What did you say, Perks? Oh, kit. Yes. The getaway bag. Nothing else. Just the getaway bag, haha! Private joke between Perks and me, Doc. Learned the ropes last time, didn't we, Perks? No more getting caught again with no kit, no bloody kit, no washanshave ten days, ten bloody days, no wash, no shave. Special haversack, we decided. Paint name on it, labels no good, they come off. Paint name big, put in books, towel, soap, socks, shave-kit, toothbrush. All in special haversack. Never to be touched, to be kept for when wounded. If wounded, tie haversack to body when they send me away. Next time we'll be wounded in luxury, we said. Oh, yes: and trousers. That's most important thing of all. Not going to be caught again in Algiers with one trouser leg – no fear, no bloody fear.

'The getaway bag, Perks,' was what he said, emerging from his delirium.

'It's outside, sir. Ready packed. Was there anything else, sir?'

'Trousers, too?'

'Yes, sir.'

'D'you hear that, Doc? Trousers. You don't know what it's like being in a place like Algiers with only half your trousers. But we're prepared this time, aren't we, Perks?'

'That's right, sir.'

'We know all the answers now, Doc. We'll be a *pauvre blessé* in style this time.'

'Yes, Tim.'

'Can I have a drink, Doc?'

'Only tea, Tim. Anything else would be unwise. Hold tight. This may hurt.' Sheldon stifled a cry.

'That's all. You can relax now.'

'Is it bad, Doc?'

'No, Tim. You'll be all right in a few days.'

'It's worse than my last one, isn't it?'

'A little. But it will clear up. You'll be all right.'

The Adjutant entered.

'Sorry to worry you, Tim,' he said. 'I got the story from the C.O. You did a good job. I just wanted to check over with you that I've got it straight, before I do the final report for Brigade.'

'Go ahead,' Sheldon said.

The Adjutant read in a rapid monotonous voice from a notebook:

Composition of patrol: officer, sergeant, five other ranks. Time out, 18.15: time in, 06.15.

Patrol reached White Farm without incident at 22.50. Took up position approximately 300 yards from main building. 23.00 own artillery fired concentrations. 23.05 enemy opened heavy fire on fixed lines and defensive fire tasks. Estimated enemy strength 1 battalion. Patrol prepared to withdraw. Enemy section of 1 officer 4 other ranks observed approaching. Patrol held fire till enemy within point blank range then killed all five. Identifications secured from officer. Enemy re-opened defensive fire. Patrol carried out tactical withdrawal with loss of one other rank killed, patrol commander wounded, both by mortar. 05.30 patrol attacked by low-flying enemy aircraft, identified as ME 109s, approximately half a mile east of forward Battalion positions. One other rank killed. Patrol returned without further incident.

'That's all, isn't it?'

'That's all,' Sheldon said.

'Many thanks. I hope the leg isn't too painful.'

'It's not too bad.'

'Well, I must get this thing copied out and sent off. Brigade are always belly-aching about our patrol reports being late. See you before you go. I must say I rather envy you.'

The Doctor finished bandaging.

'There you are, Tim. That should be a little more comfortable.'

'Thanks, Doc.'

'All you need now is a long sleep.'

As the stretcher was hoisted into the ambulance, the Colonel, the Adjutant, the Medical Officer, and the Batman watched and made jokes about Algiers and nurses and nights in the *kasbah*, and Sheldon joked back. As they were closing the ambulance doors he called to the Adjutant.

'Will you get hold of the home addresses of Tubbs and Tyldesley and send them on to me?' he asked. 'So I can write to their parents.'

The square, old-fashioned ambulance grumbled slowly across the grass to the road that was scarcely more than a track, to twist and bump the twelve miles to Brigade, where the Advanced Dressing Station was located. Again the long rhythm of evacuation. First the Regimental Aid Post, for the washing and dressing of the wound: thence to the Advanced Dressing Station where they would look at it, give him a lot of pills, and tie it up again. Then the railhead, and after that the Casualty Clearing Station where there were surgeons and plasma and anaesthetic: there the dirty jagged metal would be removed from his leg. Finally the hospital, far away in a different world.

The ambulance rolled and lurched. It was the old kind, like a furniture van, but it was well sprung and the ride was not uncomfortable. It was good to be riding at all, to be off the feet, the sore feet with blood in the boots, nice to ride, so tired, nice to ride.

In the command dugout the Colonel sat at the improvised table mechanically running his eye over papers which the Adjutant was placing before him for signature. Orderlies came and went. A clerk appeared and asked about a soldier's pay. The Padre thrust his head through the entrance – the face of a stage curate surmounted by a tin hat too small – to announce that he was about to visit Baker Company. Shells were falling sporadically. Outside, stripped to the waist, a signaller washed himself. The working day of a battalion in the line was proceeding as usual under a sky still winter grey. In the same dugout was the Medical Officer, smoking a pipe. The table was covered with a grey army blanket. There was nothing on it except the papers the Colonel was signing, a tin of cigarettes, and the small red collar badge which Sheldon had taken from the German officer. When the final copies of the patrol report had been finished by one of the clerks the collar badge would be sent back to Brigade with the report.

'Tim's going to be all right, isn't he, Doc?' the Colonel asked without looking up from the ammunition return he was signing.

'Yes. I think so.'

'It wasn't a very big piece, was it?'

'No. Not as these things go. It was quite nasty, though. It didn't get the bone, luckily. But there's a certain amount of shock. I don't think we shall see him back for some time.'

'Tim's tough,' the Colonel said, continuing to sign. 'Tougher than he looks.'

'Oh, yes. He should be all right. I must say he seemed very cheerful, considering.'

'If it had been really bad I don't suppose he could have walked in like that.'

The Doctor continued to puff at his pipe, the ascetic face set in a frown.

'I suppose,' he said after a while, 'that it was worth it?'

'How d'you mean?'

'Losing a good officer and two good men for – that!' he pointed to the German collar patch on the table.

'The job had to be done.'

'I don't know anything about tactics. But wasn't it asking for trouble to send a small patrol on a job like that? Surely the place was bound to be heavily defended?'

'Division didn't seem to think so.'

'I rather gathered that Tim did.'

'It isn't as simple as that, Doc. As you well know.'

'I suppose I'm just a fool civilian. But a lot of these patrols strike me as being rather silly. It seems a damned wasteful way of finding out whether a probable enemy strongpost is occupied in strength.'

'It's the only way. Unless one is lucky enough to pick up a talkative deserter from the other side. And then you can't be certain.'

'I suppose, Colonel, that what gets me is that it always seems to be the best ones that are – frittered away on these things.'

'Only the best ones can do them. If they hadn't been the best last night nobody would have got back. I feel as badly about it as you, Doc. But they wanted the job done, and we had to do it. Don't forget we can have casualties here any time, any day, from the shelling. It's an occupational hazard. The Messerschmitts that picked them up also strafed two of our companies this morning.'

'I hope the Brigadier was duly appreciative. Did he have much to say?'

'He said, "Good show!"'

'What a man!' the Doctor snapped. 'I think his entire range of expression is covered by "good show" and "bad show". If you told him the second coming of Christ had happened I doubt whether he could manage anything more than a tired "Good show!"'

'You mustn't be so bitter, Doc,' the Colonel said, laughing and handing the last of the papers to the Adjutant.

The Adjutant shouted to the clerk to hurry up with the patrol report. A voice from outside called back that it was nearly finished.

'I know how you feel about Tim, Doc,' the Colonel said quietly. 'He'd had more than his share.' He lit a cigarette and smoked it thoughtfully. The clerk came in with the patrol report, which he handed to the Adjutant. When he had read and signed it the Adjutant put it in an envelope together with the German collar patch and told the clerk to see that it went off to Brigade by D.R. right away. As the D.R.'s motor-cycle started up the Colonel yawned and stretched.

'Put a note in Orders tonight,' he said to the Adjutant. 'Captain Ainsworth to go up to Acting-Major and to assume command of Charlie Company.'

Alone in the ambulance Sheldon could at last enjoy the bliss, almost an ecstasy, which comes at the moment of final surrender to fatigue: a thrumming in the brain, a sensuous draining from the body and the limbs of the last drops of resisting strength. While the wound was being dressed he had relaxed, had begun to taste again the privileged helplessness of the wounded. But while he was there he could not surrender; he was still a part of something, a part of other people. He was still the commander of a company, a man with work to finish, a report to complete. Not until now, in the solitude of the ambulance could he surrender lingeringly, deliciously to total weariness. He lay in one of the lower positions staring at the brown canvas of the empty stretcher above him, swaying and lurching with the movement of the ambulance, brown canvas gently moving, lulling tired eyes that stared up from below, welcoming now the enveloping finality of fatigue...

He had reached the end of the long thin night. Now it was day, the brilliant African day. Not the grey Africa called The Battalion, but where the sun was shining. He was walking on the yellow-pink plain from which the mountains rose stark and beautiful, the mountains of North Africa he knew so well: the long, low ones fin-crested like mammoth fossilised fishes: the sharp, high ones, purple, pink or grey – with escarpments planted jauntily on their crowns. The most brilliant and graceful and prominent of them all was Piecrust and that was the one to which he was walking. His feet no longer ached as he pushed them one past the other in the rhythm of the infantry. Without pain, without sound, scarcely touching the ground, he walked towards Piecrust in the morning sunshine, passing along the plain between the naked solitary mountains.

What cosmic upheavals how many million years ago left them like this? Was this once the ocean bed and were those mountains submerged rocks to trap the Stone Age mariner? Was it the sea which washed the escarpments into their neat laminated moulds? Or some mighty glacier? The ocean. It must have been the ocean, I am walking on the waves of an ocean that is land, left right, keep moving, left right, the rhythm of the infantry, walking to Piecrust.

Ahead a figure beckoned, as he drew closer he saw that it was the girl from the Oulad Naïl, the naughty Mona Lisa, she is only thirteen but looks eighteen, Piecrust is where she lives. She beckoned and he walked towards her, forcing one foot past the other knowing that he must not stop, the only unforgivable thing is to stop, you must never stop, he must keep on for ever until he reached Piecrust and the Oulad Naïl girl, but all of a sudden she was no longer there, only Piecrust remained. The great mountain was still there, and he kept walking because he knew he must not stop.

To march without feeling, without hurting, is bliss, he marched as if on tiptoes through the dusty white plain towards the mountain that came no nearer, but he mustn't give up, must keep going one foot past the other in the rhythm of the infantry – must keep going for ever to the mountain. Piecrust was now a pinkish-blue, the colours always change in this light. He walked past an old Arab, squatting immobile, the brown hawk-like face a graven symbol of permanence; his white burnous hanging with natural grace, whichever way they hang is graceful, sculpturesque grace of robes in Michelangelo frescoes. The white folds of the burnous dissolved and became an image in a hospital ward, Sister Murgatroyd noiselessly floating, and now she was leading him to Piecrust where he had to go, dear sublime Sister Murgatroyd, wide grey eyes leading to the mountain, she was the spirit of the pink-blue mountain Piecrust, and that was where he had to go. This is what it was all for, for Sister Murgatroyd. Dear Sister Murgatroyd – my mistress, my mother, my god. I love you for ever and ever, bend low and cool the hot brow, the soft rustle of skirts is strengthening, I am so weak, marching for ever in emptiness. As he walked and walked he felt the infinite sadness of space and his eyes filled with tears, so he continued to walk and his feet no longer touched the ground and he knew he would never reach the mountain, it was to Sister Murgatroyd that he was going, to the satin shoulder, to the immemorial breast, to the full lips for kissing, to the womb to possess and be possessed. Sister Murgatroyd is strength and love and beauty and that is where I am going. I have passed through the end of the long thin night, and there is only Sister Murgatroyd. For this, through pain, I have learned: there is nothing that matters but to love and to dream. The illusion is everything, the reality nothing. Keep going, never stop, keep going, in the rhythm of the infantry one foot past the other, through the sadness of space to the high pink mountain – to the dream that is Sister Murgatroyd. For to dream is all...

In the command dugout they sat down to breakfast. The Colonel and the Doctor shared the small table, the Adjutant ate off his knee.

'What do you think the chances are, Colonel, that the Division really will get this rest they've talked about?'

'I don't know,' the Colonel said through a mouthful of sausage.

'I thought they were supposed to be organising a leave centre.'

'There was talk of it. You know how they are.'

'They'll have to do something about it soon. Otherwise the old hands are going to crack up.'

The telephone buzzed, the Adjutant reached for the receiver.

'I'm beginning to envy old Tim,' the Colonel said.

'Yes. That seems the only way a man can get a rest in this division.'

'He certainly earned it the hard way. But at least he can look forward to a nice rest now.'

'A long rest, I'm afraid, sir,' the Adjutant interrupted quietly. 'That was Brigade. Tim died in the ambulance on the way there.'

'Died? Died? What do you mean, died?' the Colonel said. 'He can't have. He was all right when he left here.' He turned to the Doctor accusingly. 'He was all right when he left here, wasn't he, Doc? How could he have died? It wasn't a bad wound. How could he have died? Just like that, Doc?'

'You can't tell,' the Doctor said. 'It might have been gas gangrene. It could have been shock. The wound itself wasn't particularly bad. A few weeks ago he would probably have taken it in his stride. But he was exhausted. He was keeping going by will-power. In that state anything can happen. I keep on saying this and it doesn't do any good. There's a certain amount of stuff in a man and when it's gone, it's gone. Tim Sheldon was – used up. Just used up.'

TEN

TEN O'CLOCK in the morning, the same day, Tuesday. At Brigade the Brigadier walked across to his private Elsan to relieve himself. He relieved himself punctually at this time every morning.

At Division Puttenham-Brown walked round the anteroom of the mess, pecking at the *Tatlers*. Then he walked over to a wall, straightened two of the Peter Scotts and flicked some dust off Mr. Churchill's nose. After that he walked across to the General's office. The Captain was in a peevish mood. After all his trouble in going to Thibar for that wine, not a single officer had remarked on it. It really was a waste of time trying to run a civilised mess for people like these.

'I see you were a bit astray in your theory that White Farm had been evacuated,' the General greeted him breezily, scratching his left buttock with zest.

'Yes, sir. You saw the report?'

'Yes, I did. It seems the place is still thick with Boche. The patrol had a good battle. They had casualties, though. Including the officer. A pity. Still, I suppose it's as well to have checked up.'

'Yes, sir. By the way, sir, how did you like the new wine?'

General Scratcher Doyle smiled dazzlingly.

'Y'know, Putt, I'm terribly sorry, but it didn't seem to me any different from the last lot.'

At Corps a plump full colonel of the Ordnance Corps glared at an indent and shouted:

'What the hell do they *do* with their boots? They can't get through that number just *walking* in them?'

At Army there was an atmosphere of strained, rather sullen eagerness brought on by a general rebuke the night before on the subject of slovenly appearance and saluting.

At Allied Forces Headquarters in Algiers the daily deluge of paper flooded the pending baskets and overflowed into the corridors.

In a club in St. James's Street, London, an old man opened his newspaper and querulously read the communiqué from Algiers. It said, simply:

'Nothing to report. Patrol activity.'

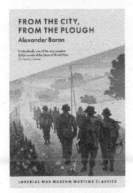

ISBN 9781912423071

£8.99

'Alexander Baron's *From the City, From the Plough* is undoubtedly one of the very greatest British novels of the Second World War and provides the most honest and authentic account of front line life for an infantryman in North West Europe.'

ANTONY BEEVOR

ISBN 9781912423163

£8.99

'Few other novels of the war describe the grinding claustrophobia, violence and lethal danger of being in a tank crew with the stark vividness of Peter Elstob... a forgotten classic that deserves to be read and read.'

JAMES HOLLAND

ISBN 9781912423095

£8.99

'Takes you straight back to Blitzed London... boasts everything a great whodunit should have, and more.'

ANDREW ROBERTS

ISBN 9781912423088
£8.99

'A tremendous rediscovery of a brilliant novel. Extremely well-written, its effects are both sophisticated and visceral. Remarkable.'

WILLIAM BOYD

ISBN 9781912423101
£8.99

'Much more than a novel'

RODERICK BAILEY

'I loved this book, and felt I was really there'

LOUIS de BERNIÈRES

'One of the greatest adventure stories of the Second World War'

ANDREW ROBERTS